SWEET AND VICIOUS

An IN or OUT Novel

BY CLAUDIA GABEL

IN or OUT

LOVES ME, LOVES ME NOT
An IN or OUT Novel

SWEET AND VICIOUS
An IN or OUT Novel

FRIENDS CLOSE, ENEMIES CLOSER
An IN or OUT Novel

SWEET AND VICIOUS

An IN or OUT Novel by
CLAUDIA GABEL

Point

ISBN-13: 978-0-439-91856-5
ISBN-10: 0-439-91856-1

Copyright © 2008 by Claudia Gabel
All rights reserved. Published by Scholastic Inc.

SCHOLASTIC and associated logos are trademarks and/or registered trademarks of Scholastic Inc.

Text design by Steve Scott
The text type was set in Bulmer.

12 11 10 9 8 7 6 5 4 3 2 1   8 9 10 11 12 13/0

Printed in the U.S.A.
First printing, January 2008

For my sister, Luci,
a friend to the end

Chapter 1

Nola James had been standing on Weston Briggs's cardboard box–filled porch for ten minutes before realizing that she hadn't rung the doorbell. In fact, she hadn't so much as moved since she'd climbed up the steps and set her Skechers-clad feet on the dirty welcome mat. Nola wasn't sure if it was fear keeping her from making her presence known or . . . okay, it was definitely fear. What made Nola think that she could hatch some mean-spirited *Punk'd*-style plot against her ex-best-friend-turned-nemesis Marnie Fitzpatrick, run next door to the house newly occupied by Marnie's former boyfriend, and expect to go through with it?

Nola let out a heavy sigh, turned on her heel, and retreated a few paces. When she reached the edge of the porch, she turned her gaze upward and looked at the evening sky. The stars were twinkling like glitter above the city of Poughkeepsie as a chilly autumn breeze kicked up piles of raked leaves in the yard. Nola zipped up her navy blue Columbia windbreaker and put her hands in her pockets, thinking about what she would do if she ever got up the nerve to ring that doorbell.

She'd concocted a basic three-pronged plan on the walk over here, which had taken her no more than thirty seconds. The first stage called for telling Weston that Marnie had just seen him from Nola's bedroom window and sent her out to ask him to meet her at Stewart's Ice Cream Shoppe tomorrow night. The second stage called for Nola convincing Marnie to work on their English project together at Stewart's tomorrow after school. The third stage called for lurking outside of Stewart's to watch a stunned Marnie come face-to-face with Weston, the boy who'd thrown Marnie's heart into a wood chipper last year (metaphorically speaking, of course).

However, two of the three stages involved trickery, and that seemed to be everyone's specialty but Nola's. She was terrible at being deceitful and always cracked under the pressure. Actually, Nola could recall about twenty different instances (including one involving Marnie, stolen thongs, and a sales clerk at Victoria's Secret) when her back was against the wall and she had to tell a half-truth, only to be betrayed by her quivering bottom lip and her infamous hive outbreaks.

This is ridiculous. There's no way I can pull this off.

Suddenly, the porch light flicked on, and Nola's breath caught in her throat. She turned around and saw Weston Briggs in the door frame, smirking as if he'd just caught Nola coming out of the shower with only a towel wrapped around her.

"I'm not one hundred percent sure, but I think you're trespassing," he said.

While Nola never understood why Marnie was so hung up on Weston, now that she was standing less than ten feet away from him, she could see what all the fuss was about. Even though he was wearing a ratty orange baseball jersey and a dingy pair of jeans, Weston was the spitting image of Heath Ledger after batting practice. His blond hair was damp with perspiration, and his big blue eyes were focused intensely on Nola, which made her extremely self-conscious. She hadn't even bothered to put on any lip gloss before she left her house. Not that it mattered what Weston thought of her. After all, Nola was a girl on a mission (except at the moment the only thing she could remember about the mission was that it had prongs).

"So, Nola, are you going to tell me why you're here, or am I going to have to guess?" Weston asked as he swaggered onto the porch and shut the door behind him.

Nola steadied herself and swallowed hard. She couldn't act nervous or Weston might suspect that she was up to no good. "I came to welcome you to the neighborhood."

Weston moved a stray box out of his path with his foot. "You live around here?"

"Right next door, actually," Nola said, gesturing to her large but quaint Victorian house, which appeared rather ominous in the dark.

"Small world," he said flatly. "Did you bring a basket of cookies or something?"

Nola let out a huff. Weston had dated her best friend for four whole months and *this* was the kind of response she got after not seeing him for almost a year? Nola hadn't expected a bear hug, but still.

"All I have is gum," she said as she pulled a pack of cinnamon Trident out of her jacket pocket.

"Cool, thanks," Weston said, snatching it out of her hand.

Ick. Why did Marnie give this guy the time of day?

Weston took a piece of gum out of its wrapper and placed it ever so seductively on his tongue.

Okay. Maybe I know why.

"So why did your family move back to Poughkeepsie?" Nola asked, hoping this would keep her from ogling Weston as he chewed.

"Eh, you know how it is," he said with a shrug.

Nola was completely baffled. "Yeah, I guess."

"How's Marnie doing?"

Nola gulped. This was the perfect opportunity to launch her scheme, which thankfully came flooding back at the mention of Marnie's name. However, as

Weston continued to chomp on her Trident, Nola began to have second thoughts. Sure, Marnie deserved to be shoved off her self-righteous pedestal after everything she'd done to Nola — ditching her for Lizette Levin and her crew of mindless Majors, accusing Nola of vandalizing her posters, and baiting Nola into a tigress fight at that stupid party on Saturday night, to name just a few evil things. But if Nola put this sneaky plan into motion, wouldn't she be sinking to Marnie's level?

Filled with doubt, Nola peered down at her sneakers and mumbled, "She's okay."

Weston chuckled. "I gotta admit, I'm surprised you two are still friends."

Nola's head snapped up. "What do you mean?"

"I know how you girls used to fight over me," Weston said with a wink. "You think I'm a dumb jock and a heartbreaker, huh?"

Nola could feel all of her appendages going numb. Back when Marnie first started going out with Weston, she and Nola had gotten into some low-grade spats over Weston's lack of smarts. Nola had also warned Marnie several times that he seemed kind of shady and would probably do her wrong, but Marnie never listened. Apparently, she'd never kept her mouth shut, either! How could Marnie sell Nola out like that even *before* Lizette Levin had come on the scene?

That's it. Marnie Fitzpatrick is going down. AND HARD!

"As a matter of fact, I do," Nola said, putting her hands on her hips in an attempt to steady herself. "But that's not important. When Marnie saw you from my bedroom window a few minutes ago, she was sobbing. She's still not over you, Weston." Nola let out a deep breath.

Weston dashed over to the side of the porch, leaned on the railing, and glanced up in the direction of Nola's window. "Really? She's *crying*?"

Nola grinned. "Like a colicky baby."

"I just saw your curtains move. She must be watching me!" Weston crowed.

Wait a minute, nobody should be in my room.

Nola hightailed it over to Weston and peered up at her bedroom window. Not only did the curtains move again, but the light also switched off. At first, Nola thought that her little brothers, Dennis and Dylan, might have been playing hide-and-seek in there, but when she cast her eyes on the kitchen window she could see both of them flinging food at each other with their spoons. That left one other person.

Ian Capshaw, Vassar College freshman and the James family manny.

"Wow, I had no idea Marnie was so . . . obsessive," Weston said, clearly impressed.

"Me neither," Nola murmured.

What was Ian doing in my room?

Weston ran his hands through his hair and took a whiff of his baseball jersey. "Maybe I should go over to your place and say hi."

Nola ripped her thoughts away from Ian and forced herself to stay on course. "Actually, Marnie wanted me to ask you if you'd meet her tomorrow night at Stewart's. She really wants to see you . . . and treat you to some gelato, if you know what I mean."

"I think I can swing that." Weston smiled widely.

"Great," Nola replied as she tucked her brown hair behind her ears and took another glimpse at her window.

Now, on to stage two.

Five minutes later, Nola was flying around her room, making sure none of her high-risk personal items had been disturbed. Thankfully, her old-fashioned but broken (yikes!) lock-and-key diary was safely tucked inside a decrepit Connect Four box in the far reaches of her closet, and her yellow Mead five-subject notebook with all the Matthew Thomas Heatherlys written on the back cover was in her overstuffed JanSport, which was near the floor of her bed — exactly where she'd left it.

Nola exhaled a small sigh of relief and sat down on her desk chair, zapped of all her energy. However, she felt a sharp pain rise in her chest when she realized that her computer was on. What if Ian had been reading her e-mails? Not that there was anything scandalous lurking in her in-box, but still — a teenage girl had to protect her right to privacy at all costs, especially when it was being invaded by a pain-in-the-ass seventeen-year-old male babysitter!

Nola held her breath as she jiggled her mouse and her kitschy Hannah Montana screen saver dissipated to reveal her e-mail account. Everything seemed in order, except that one new message had arrived.

to: *Nola James*
from: *Matt Heatherly*
subject: *Forgive me?*

Even though she'd been both really worried *and* annoyed by Matt's sudden disappearance, Nola could feel her body go limp at the sight of his name. Luckily, the e-mail hadn't been opened. Otherwise, she might have gone berserk and kicked Ian out of the house and into orbit.

Nola put one hand on her heart and used the other to double-click.

Hey Nol,

*Sorry about leaving you hanging yesterday. I wish
I had a good excuse, but honestly, I'm very . . .
confused. There is a reason behind it and I will
tell you soon. I just can't explain everything right
now. I hope you understand and that you're not
angry, because the truth is you really mean the
world to me.*
Matt

Nola stared at Matt's e-mail for so long she almost went into a trance. *You really mean the world to me?* Was Matt finally coming around and seeing her as more than just a friend?

Nola rubbed at her eyes and then looked at the screen again. Yep, the words were still there and this wasn't a hallucination. Maybe tomorrow Matt would ride over to her house on his bike, take her to the Roosevelt Mansion for a picnic breakfast, and profess his true feelings for her! Or maybe he'd write Nola a love song this time and show up on her doorstep to sing it to her. Nola's pulse was racing as she thought of all the romantic possibilities.

"Are you busy?" a voice came from behind her.

Nola swiveled around in her desk chair and saw Mr. Nosy McSnoops-a-lot standing out in the hall.

God, why didn't I at least close my door?

"Yes, I am," Nola said curtly, crossing her arms in front of her chest.

Ian marched into her room without even bothering to ask if he was welcome. "This will only take a second."

Nola gave Ian a frosty glare. *Is this the same boy who was actually being nice earlier?*

"So, that guy next door. What's his deal?" Ian narrowed his eyes at Nola and tossed her a condescending look.

"His *deal*? What business is that of yours?" Nola's voice was crackling with anger. How dare Ian talk to her like this?

Ian rolled his eyes. "I'm in charge when your parents aren't home, remember?"

As Nola stood up, she felt her face turn hard. She had almost summoned up the courage to knock off the enormous chip Ian had on his shoulder when a goofy smirk appeared on his face.

"What's so funny?" she barked.

"Hannah Montana?" Ian replied with a chuckle. "How . . . *cute*."

Immediately, Nola's I-pity-the-fool-who-snoops-in-my-room mojo vanished into thin air.

She blushed fiercely.

"Are you through humiliating me now?" Nola muttered as she shuffled over to her bed and flopped onto her back.

Ian moved a few steps closer so he towered over Nola. Although she was completely irritated and thought he was a jerk, Nola couldn't get over how good-looking Ian was. His eyes kind of sparkled when he was being mean and the smug expression that was permanently etched on his face oftentimes made him seem . . . irresistibly hot. Not that Nola would ever admit this under oath or anything. In fact, she would rather go to jail for committing perjury.

"Listen," Ian said with a resigned sigh. "I'm just doing what I'm paid to do, keep an eye on the kids. Now, what's that guy's name and what were you two doing before?"

Nola sprang up from her bed so fast Ian jumped back a few feet. "I am *not* a kid!" she growled.

She would have stopped there, but Ian looked as though he was about to laugh rather than apologize for being such a jerk. It was more than Nola could stand. "If you must know, his name is Weston and we were talking about *what a big loser you are!* Satisfied?"

Then something shocking happened. Ian's eyes dimmed and his pompous grin transformed into a hurt frown. He just stood there, gaping at Nola until he shook himself out of his daze and walked past her briskly.

Nola swallowed hard. She'd gone way too far. "Ian, wait. I —"

"Sorry I was spying before. It won't happen again," he said before shutting the door quietly behind him and leaving Nola to wonder who she was turning into.

Chapter 2

TOP PRIORITIES FOR THE NEXT TWO WEEKS
1) Read <u>Freakonomics</u> from cover to cover and highlight all passages that relate to my new cool-as-hell job!
2) Get Lizette a "thank you for being my campaign manager" present. Maybe some cute vintage earrings or a T-shirt from the Clothes Horse?
3) Make a haircut appointment at Marlene Weber. Split ends must go!
4) Spend as much time as possible with the hottie sophomore class VP!

Marnie Fitzpatrick had never had a Monday this fantastic before. First, she'd won the freshman class treasurer spot at Poughkeepsie Central High School, which was no small feat considering all the mayhem that ensued after her flubbed assembly speech and vandalized posters. Nevertheless, the people had spoken loud and clear — they wanted Marnie to run the show, and now that she had finally solidified her standing in the Majors, that was exactly what she planned to do.

Second, her new BFF, Lizette Levin, had already begun making plans for this highly elite and hush-hush inauguration party that was invite-only and would be held at a top secret location. Marnie was thrilled to be in the center of all this hype. She couldn't wait for next Friday.

Last, but by no means least, Marnie was currently canoodling with newly elected sophomore vice president Dane Harris on his . . . wait for it . . . *king-size bed*! They were side by side, kissing through a three-hour block of *Lost* on DVD. Marnie pulled back a little, opening her eyes and casting them on Dane's exquisite face. His nose was absolutely perfect, despite the teeny bump near the bridge. His lips were red and his cheeks were pink, most likely side effects from their marathon make-out session. Marnie reached up and traced a finger along his chin, and Dane opened his eyes as though he'd been asleep for days.

"Mmmm . . . why did you stop?" he murmured into her ear.

Marnie almost shivered with joy. "I just wanted to look at you," she said through a whisper.

Dane ran his hand along the edge of Marnie's skirt. "Well, I hope you like what you see. I know I do."

Marnie took Dane's hand in hers and squeezed it tightly. She could just lie there forever, snuggled up next to him and inhaling the shower-fresh scent of his skin. And she would have, if a JoJo ringtone hadn't blared out from inside her tote bag.

"Would you kill me if I got that?" Marnie said as she pressed her lips against his neck lightly.

"I guess not," he said.

"Thanks." Marnie kissed him on his forehead and rolled over to the edge of Dane's bed. She stretched out and grabbed her bag off the floor, digging through the contents until she found her pink Razr. She smiled when she saw Lizette's name.

"Hey, Zee," Marnie answered cheerily.

"Omigod, I'm at the Galleria right now and I just spotted a dress for your party. It was so *boss*!" Lizette shrieked into the phone.

"You did?" Marnie was practically hyperventilating.

"Wait, where are you?" Lizette asked coyly. "I'm getting a strong hook-up vibe."

Marnie's eyes grew wide. Could Lizette read her mind? "Um . . . I'm at Dane's house."

Lizette laughed loudly. "I knew it! You're such a *vixen*!"

Marnie giggled as she pushed some stray blonde hairs out of her eyes with her free hand. "I am not."

"Whatever, Marn," Lizette said. "Ugh, someone's on the other line. Be right back."

"Okay."

Dane started rubbing her back with his hands, and Marnie was unable to hold in a happy sigh.

Why did I even pick up the phone?!

"Back!" Lizette chirped. "That was Brynne. She's on her way to meet me for QT."

In an instant, Marnie's happy mood plummeted below sea level. She'd put it out of her mind for the last few hours, but now that Lizette had mentioned quality time with the gap-toothed demon, all Marnie could think about was seeing that purple marker come out of Brynne's bag at lunch today. That and how maybe she'd pointed her accusatory finger at an innocent person, who also happened to be her ex-best friend.

"I better get going then." Marnie was trying hard to focus on Dane's awesome massage and nothing else.

"Yeah, don't let me ruin the mood," Lizette said with a goofy snicker. "Talk to ya later!"

"Bye," Marnie said, snapping the phone shut and tossing it on the thick gray carpet.

Dane pulled her back into his arms and kissed her cheek. "Where were we?"

Marnie remembered exactly where they were, but she was so tense her body felt like it was being twisted like an Aunt Annie's Glazin' Raisin pretzel. Her mind was on overload, too. There was no use hiding it — Marnie wasn't in the make-out zone any longer.

"Sorry, Dane," she said, edging her way out of his embrace a little.

"Is there something wrong?"

"Kind of." Marnie felt awful for letting that dirtbag Brynne come between her and a smooch-fest with Dane. But at the same time she figured that if she confided in him about the Purple Marker Crisis he'd have some advice on what to do.

Marnie rolled on her back and gazed at the ceiling fan. "It's just that I think I know who wrecked my posters."

Dane sat up. "What do you mean? I thought you said Nola did it."

"Well, earlier today, Brynne's phone went off in the cafeteria but she was getting Little Debbie snack cakes, so Grier went into her bag to silence her cell, and she pulled out a purple magic marker," Marnie explained.

"I see. And you think it's the same one that was used to deface your posters," Dane said.

"It's no secret that Brynne would love to kick my ass," Marnie said.

Dane put a hand on Marnie's knee. "True, but why would she write 'Thong Thief' on everything?"

Marnie propped herself up on her elbows and looked at Dane quizzically. He brought up a good point. How could Brynne have even known about the Thong Thief incident without Nola giving up the goods?

Oh, my God. Are Nola and Brynne working together?

It made sense, yet when Marnie really considered this possibility, she had a difficult time believing that Nola was capable of carrying out such a cunning scheme. Nola always buckled when it came to lies and scams, and Nola was way too afraid of Brynne to even think of teaming up with her. Still, how had Brynne found out?

"I don't know," Marnie replied. "Brynne seemed to enjoy watching me squirm at assembly while the whole school taunted me. Nola wasn't even there."

Dane let out a hearty laugh. "So? You were going to win that election no matter what Brynne did."

Marnie made a confused face. "Come on, Dane. You have to admit I was a little bit lucky to win in spite of what happened."

"I don't believe in luck," Dane said as he leaned in toward Marnie, drawing her backward so her head rested on a pillow. "I have friends in high places."

Dane was inches away from kissing Marnie when she slid out from underneath him and jumped off the bed.

"What'd I say?" His voice had a tinge of annoyance to it.

"Are you telling me that you *fixed the election?*" Marnie said sharply. She couldn't believe that she was accusing Dane of this, but how else did he expect her to react to what he'd said? *Gee, honey! That's wonderful?*

"I was *kidding,* Marnie," Dane huffed. "God, can't you take a joke?"

Marnie swallowed hard. "You were?"

"Yes, of course."

Holy crap. This is beyond embarrassing.

Marnie slunk back over to Dane's Ralph Lauren flannel sheet–covered bed and sat on the edge. "I guess I'm kind of paranoid, huh?"

Dane laid down on his back and put his arms behind his head. "Kind of."

Great. Now he's pissed at me.

Marnie bit her lower lip and ran her hands through her hair. The last thing she wanted to do was wreck her celebratory kissing extravaganza with Dane. Regardless of whatever drama was going on with Lizette, Brynne, and Nola, she had to make things right with her kinda-sorta boyfriend before he began scrolling through the contacts in his cell phone, looking for someone else to take her place.

Marnie crawled over to Dane and scooted right up to him so her face was close to his and he couldn't look away. "I'm sorry," she said softly, and kissed him on his chin. A moment later, Marnie moved on to a special spot on his neck where she knew he was ticklish and Dane instantly broke into a fit of laughter. Marnie chimed in, too.

"No fair! You cheated," Dane said as he reached for Marnie's feet.

"Don't you dare!" Marnie yelped.

But Dane did dare, and the tickle fight that followed made Marnie lose track of all her worries, especially when it turned into the *Lost* Make-out Session Redux.

Yet deep down she knew the paranoia would strike again, only she wasn't sure just when.

Chapter 3

On Tuesday morning, Nola sat in English class, nervously clicking her blue ink pen and listening to Marnie read a long passage aloud from their textbook. She couldn't help but notice how incredible her ex-best friend looked today. Marnie's blonde hair was pulled back into a low, loose ponytail and she was wearing a cute black sweater dress with a gigantic red belt that showed off her tiny waist. Nola also took note of how measured and confident Marnie's voice was, and how she never mispronounced a word. It was as if Marnie had built some kind of special invisible force field around her, where nothing and no one could touch her.

But Nola knew better than that. In only a few hours, Marnie would be the victim of a nasty prank. Nola had thought that once she saw Marnie and remembered all the crappy things she'd done to Nola in the past few weeks, it would be easy to initiate the second phase of her ruse. Nola had even tried to prepare this morning by practicing her lines with Dennis and Dylan as they threw handfuls of Kix everywhere. Still, here she was, minutes away from tapping Marnie on the shoulder and asking her to meet after school, and the only thing Nola could think of was . . . *Ian?*

As the memory of their confrontation played in her mind, Nola tugged on a stray string jutting out from the sleeve of her favorite forest green Esprit pullover. She recalled how hurt Ian had looked when she'd insulted him, and although she reminded herself that he'd provoked her, Nola felt awful about being that cruel. After all, Ian was right — he was just watching out for her *and* the boys, like her parents had asked him to do. Sure, he went about it in an idiotic college-boy manner, but did she really have to go bonkers on him?

Speaking of bonkers, that was precisely how Nola would characterize the plan she had to bait Marnie. Nola had only known Ian for a week or so and she seemed to be consumed with guilt over what she'd said to him. How was she going to feel after tricking Marnie, a person she'd been BFF with her whole life and shared all her secrets with? Nola had hoped that her desire to put Marnie in her place would overshadow any feelings of nostalgia, but right now, she was worried that at the last minute she'd chicken out, or worse — that in the middle of putting her diabolical scheme into motion, Nola's neck would redden, and Marnie would be onto her.

"Therefore, symbolism in a story is just as important as the characters that inhabit it." Marnie finished the last line of the chapter right before the class bell rang.

"Okay, folks, don't forget to look up your homework assignment online. I should have it posted by lunchtime," Mr. Quinn said as he stood up from behind his desk. "Oh, and the presentation list for oral reports is already available, so make sure to check that as well. Have a great day!"

As her fellow classmates gathered their things, Nola kept her eyes trained on Marnie, who picked up her tote bag and set it on her desk so she could put her books inside. But in order for Marnie to fit everything into her bag, she had to yank out a dark indigo jean jacket and throw it over her shoulders. Marnie flipped up the collar and smiled, then began filling up her bag.

Nola was surprised by how quickly her blood pressure spiked and fond memories of the past receded at the sight of that jacket. The only thing she wanted to do was show Marnie what it was like to feel betrayed.

Nola inhaled deeply and took a few steps toward Marnie, her Skechers squeaking so loudly that Marnie shifted her gaze to see who was coming toward her. Nola stopped cold when they locked eyes, but thankfully she was able to blurt out her first line without too much hesitation.

"Hey."

Marnie scowled and slung her bag over her shoulder without saying a word.

Nola was afraid that Marnie might ignore her, so afraid, in fact, that she already felt a warm, itching sensation traveling up her forearms. She had to follow up with a comment that was sincere and friendly, something that would be sure to get Marnie to talk to her.

"Nice outfit, Marn. Did you get that at T.J.Maxx?" Nola blurted out.

Okay, so that wasn't exactly what Nola had in mind, but it sure got a reaction out of Marnie, who immediately stiffened up like a starched collar and pursed her lips tightly. Nola swallowed hard and tried to remember what came next in the script.

"At least I don't shop at Hobby House and sit home all day making *lame-ass* jewelry," Marnie snapped.

All right, forget the script. Nola was not about to take any crap from someone who actually used to *beg* her to make jewelry. How dare she make fun of Nola after all the gorgeous pieces she'd given Marnie over the years?

"At least I have *skills* and *talent*. You're not good at anything, except for *backstabbing*."

Instead of retaliating, Marnie mumbled an indifferent "Whatever" and darted out the door.

As Nola hurried through the hall to her next class, trembling, she chastised herself for even thinking she could coax Marnie into a trap. They were enemies, for

God's sake! How would Nola ever be able to lure Marnie anywhere when they couldn't even be nice to each other for more than a nanosecond?

Nola pulled out her cell from her jeans pocket and text-messaged Weston to abort the plan.

SOMETHING CAME UP W/MF. 2NITE IS OFF. TALK LATER. — N

This is hopeless, Nola thought as she hit the SEND button.

"Can I escort you to your destination, Miss James?" a voice bellowed out from the crowd.

Nola turned around and saw Matt Heatherly making his way through the group of students. He was wearing a navy blue waffle-knit Henley and a pair of faded black jeans. From the looks of his hair, Matt had gotten up late and hadn't bothered to comb it. As soon as he was within two feet of her, Nola nearly lost her breath.

Completely hopeless.

"Where are you off to?" Matt asked with a grin.

At the moment, Nola could barely remember the name of the school they attended. Although she knew it started with a capital *P.*

"Uh . . . um . . . social studies," Nola faltered.

"Ah, with the ever so wise Mr. Jenkins, I presume."
Matt cleared his throat. "*'You can kid your parents. You can
kid your teachers. You can even kid the board of regents. But
good God, don't kid yourself.'*"

Nola laughed at Matt's spot-on imitation. "How
long have you been working on that?"

"Too long, apparently," he said.

Nola shivered with excitement as Matt's arm
brushed against hers when they wriggled through the
packed hall. Her botched plan far from her mind, she
was wishing Matt would whisk her off to the airport
and hire a jet to fly them to a villa in Italy, or at the very
least compliment her on the ruby stone pendant she'd
made last night and was wearing on a chain around her
neck. (She wasn't too picky.)

"So what are you doing for lunch today?" Matt
asked.

"The usual," she said, pausing outside Mr. Jenkins's
classroom.

Matt put his books under his right arm and shoved
his left hand in his pocket. "How do you feel about dining outside on the bleachers near the football field with
yours truly?"

It's not a villa in Italy, but . . .

"Great!" she replied with enthusiasm.

Matt chuckled. "You don't get out much, do you?"

Nola knew that Matt was kidding, but she felt as though he'd just stomped on her foot. She peered down at her Skechers to make sure that he hadn't. When the bell for the next class rang, Nola looked back up and Matt had already started down the hall.

"See you at noon," he called over his shoulder.

Nola was still too embarrassed by his comment to do anything but wave. She turned and took a step toward the classroom, asking herself if she'd read way too much into Matt's e-mail.

"Nola!"

She spun around quickly and saw Matt standing at the far end of the hall, his hands cupping his mouth so that he could project his voice far and wide.

"That necklace is hot!" he shouted.

Nola's cheeks turned bright red, and luckily, there was no chance Matt saw it.

"Thanks!" she shouted back.

When Matt disappeared around the corner, Nola stood in that spot dreamily until Mr. Jenkins called out from behind and told her to get to class. However, for the next forty-five minutes, the only thing Nola could think of was how Matt had never mentioned the e-mail he had sent her, but instead had looked into her eyes and said, *"Don't kid yourself."*

Chapter 4

At midday, Marnie was sitting on a floor mat in the gymnasium, trying to rid herself of the anger that her run-in with Nola had stirred up. While she was having a hard time believing that Nola had found the nerve to pick a fight out of nowhere, Marnie was having an even *harder* time believing that she backed down with a weak "whatever" when Nola had her on the ropes.

Sure, she'd been taken aback by Nola's surprise jab, but there was no excuse for the way she'd fled the scene. It had made Marnie look like she believed what Nola had said about her being a backstabber, and that couldn't be further from the truth! Marnie hadn't done anything to Nola except try to help her get in good with the Majors. Was it *her* problem that Nola would rather sit on the sidelines and mope herself to death instead?

Hell, no!

The only issue Marnie cared to focus on right now was deciding between ensembles for her inauguration bash. As Lizette and company huddled in a secluded corner of the gym, waiting for their ginseng-popping elderly physical fitness teacher, Grams, to show up with her megaphone, Lizette talked about the headway she'd made with the party plans since last night. Not only did

Lizette have the guest list (which included every Major in each grade) all ready, but she also had the venue picked — Grier's sprawling estate near Locust Grove, the Samuel Morse historic site, where Grier's philanthropic, socialite mother was a volunteer tour guide.

"You won't believe this, Marn," Lizette said as she tightened the laces of her magenta Adidas, which clashed with the colors of her polyester uniform (of course). "Grier found a secret way onto the grounds so we can sneak in!"

Marnie put her hands over her mouth and gasped.

"How cool would it be to see the mansion and the gardens at night?" Grier beamed as she pushed down her white crew socks.

"Is this a field trip or a party?" Brynne snorted after biting off a hangnail.

Lizette bolted upright and sneered. "Excuse me?"

Immediately, Brynne's demeanor softened. "What I meant to say was, I doubt people are going to care about seeing the mansion. We've been there a bunch of times and, I don't know, it's kind of boring."

Marnie rolled her eyes at Brynne's pathetic backpedaling. "Well, I think it's fantastic, Zee."

"You would," Brynne said sarcastically.

When is this brat going to stop running her stupid mouth? Marnie thought angrily. Brynne made a point of dumping on Marnie every chance she got, and when it came down to being bitter and vindictive, Brynne was a pro. It was pretty clear that she'd had plenty of motivation to sabotage the election for Marnie.

But before Marnie could finish profiling Brynne, Grier leaped up off her mat, took Marnie by the hands, and pulled her up to her feet. "I'm so excited! I bet this party is going to be even better than the Homecoming dance."

Suddenly, a jolt of nervous energy rushed through Marnie's circulatory system. The Homecoming dance was on the horizon — about three weeks away — and although she technically had a kinda-sorta boyfriend, Dane hadn't asked her to the dance yet. It was a bit worrisome.

"Why did you have to mention that retarded dance?" Lizette grumbled as she stood and stretched her arms above her head.

"You're not looking forward to Homecoming?" Marnie was surprised.

Brynne came to Lizette's side and nodded her head in agreement. "Who is? It's a dumb, lame tradition and only the Minors, Leeks, and other nobodies go to it."

Lizette put her hands on her hips. "Is *that* what you think, Brynne? I was just stressed about what I was going to wear."

Marnie smirked. There was no way Brynne could backpedal out of *this* one.

"I . . . um, well . . ." Brynne stammered as she wrung her hands.

Lucky for Brynne, sweet and cheery Grier graciously changed the subject. "Boo-hoo, Zee! I'm stressed about *getting a date*. What if nobody asks me?" she said with a cute pout.

"Are you kidding? Boys are going to *pounce* on you," Marnie said, pinching Grier on her arm.

Lizette scooped up her sleek blonde hair, twisted it tightly, and fastened it to the back of her head with a white plastic clip. "I'm with Grier. The guy situation *sucks*."

Marnie was stunned again. Since when did *Lizette* have problems in the boy department?

"Shhh! He's coming," Grier whispered.

"Who is?" Brynne mumbled.

The skin above Lizette's upper lip was suddenly damp. "Everybody just ignore him."

Marnie glanced over Lizette's shoulder, catching a glimpse of Poughkeepsie Central's ultimate skateboard stud, Sawyer Lee. He was strolling through the gym with two members of his slacker posse, probably on his way to the track where the boys were having their PE class. He was wearing a black Zoo York T-shirt and camouflage cutoff shorts with deep-red Vans. His glossy black hair was soft and product-free today, and his smile was as devastating as ever.

Marnie put her hand on her fluttering stomach, took a deep breath, and reminded herself that Sawyer Lee was still number two on her Crush List. Number *two*. And he was Lizette's boy toy anyway, so that meant Marnie had to forget about Sawyer's wry smile, sexy swagger, and his dark, penetrating eyes. Only that would be like failing to recall the Pledge of Allegiance. How could she forget something that she didn't even remember learning?

Lizette wasn't having trouble pretending that Sawyer didn't exist, though. She was too busy immersing herself in some ridiculous fake conversation with Brynne and Grier. But as soon as Sawyer was out of sight-and-hearing range, Lizette put their chat to a halt with an annoyed sigh.

"I can't believe he didn't come over here to say hi," Lizette said, exasperated. "I have no idea what his malfunction is, but it's getting old *real fast*."

"You should just dump that poseur and move on," Brynne barked.

"Maybe I should," Lizette said, a sly grin appearing on her rosy-cheeked face. "Actually, I have my sights set on another yummy guy."

Marnie had to rub her temples counterclockwise in order to prevent her cranium from exploding.

Oh, my God! Did Zee just say she might break up with Sawyer and *that she was into* someone else?

But before Marnie could get any clarification, a loud voice filled the stuffy gymnasium air.

"TOP OF THE MORNIN' TO YA, LASSIES!"

Marnie and the rest of her classmates spun around and came face-to-bullhorn with aviator glasses–wearing Grams. Everyone began squinting simultaneously because Grams had traded in her snazzy velour sweat suit for something a little less flattering — a cotton-spandex one in blinding neon yellow.

"WHAT'S WITH ALL YOUR STRANGE FACES?" Grams asked. She looked down at her clipboard and then back up at her students. "LINE UP FOR ROLL AND THEN AFTER THAT BREAK INTO TEAMS OF NINE. WE'RE GOING TO PLAY SOME VOLLEYBALL!"

Now? Marnie hadn't gotten to the bottom of anything yet! She didn't know if Lizette was really serious about cutting Sawyer loose or who this other "yummy" guy was. This was critical information that could have serious ramifications on her life! Couldn't a sensible woman like Grams understand that?

"MOVE YOUR KEESTERS, GALS, OR I'LL TAKE OUT MY DENTURES AND FLAP MY GUMS!"

I guess not, Marnie thought as her classmates groaned in disgust.

Everyone clustered into a few groups of nine, with Marnie, Lizette, Brynne, and Grier joining forces with three Jockettes and a couple of Leeks. Grams had the teams arrange themselves on either side of three nets, gave them the game rules, and then blew her whistle — into the megaphone.

Marnie pulled her fingers out of her ears when she got up to the net. As she waited for her team to serve the ball to their opponents, she jogged in place and limbered up, visualizing herself spiking the ball to score the first point. But her mental exercises came to a screeching halt when she was hit in the shoulder by a speeding volleyball.

Marnie stumbled forward, managing to grab hold of the net and prevent herself from wiping out entirely. When she whipped around, she saw Brynne near the service line, chuckling just like the villain in a *Pirates of the Caribbean* movie.

"Oops," Brynne said, her voice oozing with sarcasm. "Don't I get a second serve, Marnie?"

Oh, it is SO FREAKING ON!

Marnie stormed over to Brynne angrily, her highly unfashionable shorts riding up her butt with each furious stride. She stopped right in front of her nemesis and held up a fist to Brynne's face. "How would you like that gap between your teeth to be *ten feet wider*?"

Brynne didn't even flinch. In fact, she just laughed. "That is the weakest threat I've ever heard."

"It won't be so weak when you're in the hospital *sipping your meals through a straw*!" Marnie snapped.

"*Guuuuys,* please don't *fiiiight*!" Grier warbled.

Marnie stepped back a little and looked over Grier's messy red mane to where Lizette was standing. Oddly enough, her friend was involved in conversation with one of the Jockettes, oblivious to the mega meow-down that was about to ensue. It just didn't seem fair. Wasn't Zee supposed to have Marnie's back at times like these? And how could she be a few feet away and not even notice the abuse Brynne was dishing out?

Whatever the reason, it made Marnie feel abandoned. However, as she recovered from Brynne's mighty blow with an ice pack on the sidelines, she didn't feel as bad for thinking PG-13-rated thoughts about the number two boy on her Crush List.

Chapter 5

Nola had been sitting outside on the bleachers and eating her lunch for about ten minutes when she saw Matt stroll across the football field. He was carrying a brown paper bag in his left hand and a bottle of Sunkist in his right, smiling with each step he took toward her. Nola gulped down a bite of her low-sodium Jif creamy peanut butter and organic banana sandwich and prayed that the overcast skies wouldn't give way to rain.

"Sorry, Nol," Matt said as he climbed to the top of the metallic bleachers, his long, lean legs moving quickly. "I would have been here on time but Miss Sofka held me after math class to lecture me on how messy my handwriting is."

Nola stared into Matt's eyes. Even though she was sure they were hazel, the gray sky and the navy shirt he was wearing brought out the blue in his irises. "That's okay."

"Is this seat taken?" Matt motioned to a spot close to Nola and grinned.

"Actually, I reserved it just for you," Nola said sheepishly.

That might be the dumbest thing I have ever said.

Matt brought his Sunkist up near his heart and

pretended to cry. "Oh, Nola, I am deeply moved by this grand gesture."

Nola laughed as she tossed a rolled-up napkin at him, but Matt was too quick and dodged it.

"You shouldn't litter, you know." Matt sat down next to Nola and nudged her leg with his knee. "So what's for lunch?"

Nola wanted nothing more than to lunge forward and wrap her arms around him, but instead she just held up the remaining portion of her sandwich and said, "My mom made it."

"Wait, she didn't fix you something with bean sprouts?" Matt said with a snicker. "I'm amazed."

Nola nodded at his paper bag. "So what do you have in there?"

Matt reached in and pulled out two Hostess chocolate cupcake packs. "The Heatherly residence is running low on groceries. This was all that was left in the cupboards."

Nola laughed again. "Why didn't you just pick up something from the cafeteria?"

"I'm trying to save money, that's all." Matt's face fell a bit as he tore into the cellophane wrapper of one of the cupcake packs. "It's kind of why I wanted to sit out here. I didn't want Iris and Evan asking any probing questions about my finances."

Nola slouched forward and sighed heavily. If this was why Matt asked her to have lunch on the bleachers, then she really was kidding herself about him liking her as more than a friend. But Nola's mind kept circling back to that e-mail — Matt had written that he was confused and she meant the world to him. He had to have been sincere, right? The only way to know for sure was to talk to Matt about it, and since he wasn't in any rush to bring the subject up, Nola decided that like it or not, she had to go out on a limb here.

But first she would take another bite of her sandwich. After all, shy girls like her needed their strength, especially around adorable cupcake aficionados like Matt.

"I thought the orange soda would be a good combination with the chocolate," Matt said after taking a swig of his Sunkist. "Boy was I wrong."

Nola raised her eyebrows in agreement as she tried to peel peanut butter off the roof of her mouth with her tongue.

"I was wondering about something." Matt shifted his gaze to his Converse sneakers. "Did you get that e-mail I sent you?"

Nola swallowed so hard, she was certain she strained her esophagus muscles. In fact, she could barely squeak out her response, which was a simple "Uh-huh."

Matt aimed his gaze overhead. It appeared as though he was wishing the clouds would disappear so that the sun could shine again. "I feel like there's so much to tell you and I don't even know where to begin."

Nola was taken aback by the sullen expression on Matt's face and how his mood had suddenly turned serious. It was clear that Matt wasn't about to profess his undying love for her, but right now Nola couldn't care less about that. All she wanted was for Matt to lean on her, like a best friend — or a boyfriend — would.

"You can start at the beginning," Nola said, laying a comforting hand on Matt's shoulder.

Matt turned his head and gave her a solemn smile. Then he put his bottle of Sunkist on the metal between his feet and took her hand in his. "A lot of strange stuff has happened in my life. Way too much for your average fourteen-year-old, believe me."

Nola squeezed Matt's hand. "Like what?"

Matt took a deep breath and tried to get the words out, but then he bowed his head in defeat.

It was the first time Nola had ever seen Matt this troubled and she didn't know what to do. Did this have anything to do with the police investigation that Riley had mentioned at the party? Or his suspension from middle school a while back? Or was it a family issue?

The way her heart was palpitating, Nola felt as though she'd just sprinted with the top members of the cross-country running team and lost by a thousand yards.

"I'm sorry, it's just . . . I guess I'm not ready to talk to you about this yet," Matt mumbled. "It's just too . . . personal."

Nola lowered her eyes and sighed when she saw how her fingers were entwined tightly with Matt's. It hurt so much to hear that he couldn't bring himself to confide in her, especially because she thought she'd proven herself to be worthy of his trust. But as soon as Nola caught a glimpse of the bracelet around Matt's wrist — the infamous blue rubber one that proclaimed *RF Forever* — feelings of jealousy overcame her and she snapped.

"But you could talk with *Riley* about it, *right?*"

Nola felt her mouth drop open in pure shock. *Why did I say something horrible like that?*

It was a question that she already knew the answer to, but at the same time, she felt totally clueless. Matt had every right to share his troubles with whomever he felt most comfortable, and being a jerk to him wasn't going to score Nola any points. Nola pulled her hand away from Matt's grasp as she turned her gaze to his geeky-cute face, expecting him to make an equally obnoxious remark before storming off.

Instead Matt finished the rest of his Sunkist, wiped his lips with the back of hand, and said, "She's my girlfriend, Nol."

Like I could ever forget.

Even though Nola felt as though her heart was being rubbed against a cheese grater, she still felt like she should apologize for the sharp tone she'd taken with Matt. But she'd have to compete with his cell phone, which started ringing incessantly. It was no contest, though. Matt immediately stood up, reached in his front pants pocket, checked the caller ID, and answered it.

"Hello, Dad?"

There was a long pause that made Nola very uneasy. As Matt paced back and forth nervously, she tried to finish the rest of her sandwich so it didn't look as though she was hoping to listen in on his conversation. But Nola was so keyed up that she couldn't even sip her V-8 Splash.

"Okay, I'm on my way," Matt said hurriedly, and then flipped his phone shut. "Nola, I have to split. Could you stop by the attendance office for me and tell Mrs. Elliott that I had to go home for a family emergency?"

"What's wrong?" Nola asked with concern.

"Can't get into it now." Matt grabbed his things and began bounding down the bleachers, taking them two at a time. When he got to the bottom, he spun around and called out to Nola, "You should see the nurse while you're at it. Your hives are back again."

queenzee: *hola, m!*

marniebird: *hey, zee! whazzup?*

queenzee: *just got home from yoga, but i don't feel centered!* ☹

marniebird: *oh, no! why not?*

queenzee: *this sawyer thing is bugging me out. he didn't even talk 2 me in homeroom!*

marniebird: *ick, that really sucks*

queenzee: *i just don't understand, why is he being such an a-hole?*

marniebird: *wish i knew, maybe there's a rational explanation*

queenzee: *doubt it*

marniebird: *well, why don't u focus on good things 4 now? like this yummy morsel u mentioned! ;-)*

queenzee: *omg, he is soooo boss, the definition of eye candy*

marniebird: *who is he?!?!*

queenzee: *that's 4 me 2 know and u 2 find out*

marniebird: *oh u r so whack!*

queenzee: *LOL*

queenzee: *here's a hint. he's an upperclassman*

marniebird: *um, that doesn't narrow it down much*

queenzee: *ok, 1 more. he's a leek!*

marniebird: *ugh, worst hints ever*

queenzee: *i like 2 keep people guessing*

marniebird: *that's an understatement*

queenzee: *so u want 2 go shopping 4 Homecoming dresses tonight?*

marniebird: *i'd like 2, but i'd feel kind of weird cuz I haven't gotten asked officially*

queenzee: *oh please, like DH would ask anyone else!*

marniebird: *well i don't want 2 assume anything*

queenzee: *c'mon, marn. he's crazy about u*

marniebird: *if u say so ;-)*

queenzee: **sigh* since u don't want 2 shop, want 2 chill at cubbyhole? it's open mike nite*

marniebird: *sure! meet u there at 6:30*

queenzee: *great, if ur good i'll give u more hints later!*

marniebird: *yay! c u soon*

queenzee: *c ya!*

Chapter 6

Early on Tuesday evening, Marnie dashed down Raymond Avenue at full throttle, hoping the kitten heels on her black, knot-front Seychelles wouldn't snap right off. It was already 6:45 and there were still seven more blocks between her and the Cubbyhole Coffeehouse. After her IM conversation with Lizette, Marnie had decided to change into a pair of gray stovepipe jeans (which she'd bought at the Gap for half price because of a tear in the back pocket). However, she'd spent way too long searching for her favorite red V-neck tunic top and now she was late!

With each steadfast stride, Marnie could feel her ponytail waving back and forth as her feet pounded the pavement. The rhythm reminded her of how clear her mind became during her morning jogs. At the moment, though, Marnie's thoughts were going a trillion miles per minute. She was still smarting from Brynne's blatant volleyball attack and how Lizette was oblivious to it. On top of that, Marnie had been stressing over Lizette and her fresh boy meat. Why was she holding out on Marnie with more specific details on this new guy? Didn't Lizette trust her? Best friends told each other secrets, so if Lizette wasn't confiding in Marnie, maybe they weren't as close as Marnie thought.

Once the Cubbyhole Coffeehouse came into view, Marnie slowed to a walk. She caught her breath and straightened out her tunic so that she wouldn't look like a complete wreck. Then Marnie halted for a minute so she could reapply her hot-pink Smashbox lip gel. As she dug through the contents of her bag in search of the sparkly tube, she heard a familiar laugh that made her glance up.

Standing right underneath the Cubbyhole sign, which was in the shape of a large orange coffee mug, were Lizette and Dane, giggling uncontrollably. Marnie's eyes widened when she saw Lizette bury her head in Dane's chest while he affectionately wrapped an arm around her.

Okay, I must have broken a blood vessel in my brain. That is the only logical explanation for this.

Suddenly, Dane looked in Marnie's direction and smiled as though Lizette wasn't pressed up against him. He tapped Lizette on the shoulder and pointed at Marnie. In her plaid miniskirt, white knee-high stockings, and shiny bright-blue geisha-inspired top that bared her middriff, Lizette was the epitome of sexy cool.

And still in Marnie's kinda-sorta boyfriend's arms.

"Thank God, you finally showed up!" Lizette called out as she skipped toward Marnie. "I was getting lonely."

Marnie's cute shoes were glued to the concrete beneath her. What was Dane even doing here? And why the hell was Lizette *flirting* with him?

Dane followed behind Lizette, his hands now safely in his pockets. "I was just in the neighborhood and spotted Lizette sitting inside all by herself, so I kept her company."

Marnie barely moved an inch when Dane gave her a soft, sweet kiss on her cheek. She felt paralyzed. Marnie tried to shake herself out of this freak-out, but all she could think about was how Lizette described her new crush — an upperclassman, a Leek. Wasn't Dane *both* of those things? Even so, it wasn't as if Marnie had just caught Lizette and Dane kissing or anything. Then again, she could see that Lizette's supple lips didn't have the usual two layers of gloss on them. Wasn't that a flaming red flag that they'd been lip to lip?

Whatever you do, Marn — don't lose it!

"Oh, that was nice of you," she finally managed to say.

"Well, I better get going. I was supposed to pick up some macaroni salad for my mom at Delforno's." Dane pulled Marnie into a hug and whispered into her ear, "Can't wait to sneak off with you at the mansion, babe."

Marnie didn't have a chance to reply. Dane took off down the street, leaving her alone with a blushing, almost giddy Lizette.

"Want to go inside? They're setting up for the open mike," Lizette said, taking Marnie's hand in hers.

"Sure."

Lizette pushed open the door and led Marnie into the coffeehouse, which was brimming with kids who were waiting to see their friends participate in a weekly amateur talent show and with older people who were reading the paper. Lizette spotted an empty couch near the far end of the purple wall, flopped down on it, and crossed her long, smooth legs at the ankles. Marnie took a seat next to her, keeping her bag on her lap.

"So guess who finally called me?" Lizette said as she raised her arm and got the attention of a waitress.

Marnie was in no mood for Lizette's guessing games.

"Sawyer Lee," Lizette added smugly.

A young woman with dark hair, knobby knees, and a freckle on her chin approached them with a pencil and a notepad. "You ladies want anything?"

Lizette twirled a strand of blonde hair around her index finger. "Um . . . I'll have a soy vanilla latte with cinnamon and some chocolate biscotti."

Knobby Knees repeated the order and wrote it down on her notepad. Then she looked at Marnie. "And what can I get for you, miss?"

"A chai tea and a couple madeleines."

"Of course," Knobby Knees said as she wobbled away.

"*Chai tea?* Who are you, Grams?" Lizette poked Marnie in the arm jokingly.

Marnie tried to laugh and pretend that seeing Lizette cozy up to Dane didn't bother her one bit, but she couldn't. There was this anger bubbling up inside of her, and she was using every shred of willpower she had to keep it from spewing everywhere.

"I think I'm getting a cold," she mumbled. *I've got to come up with a better line. It's getting old!*

"Ugh, I know. I was feeling really germy at the football game, too," Lizette said empathetically. "Thank God Sawyer let me share his coat."

Suddenly, a lightning storm erupted in Marnie's mind. Maybe this little flirt-fest between Lizette and Dane was just payback for Marnie and Sawyer's teensy go-round at the football game. It made perfect sense! Lizette was probably showing Marnie what it felt like to see her man cavorting with her good friend. And honestly, it felt like stepping in two pounds of dog poop. No wonder Lizette had been so bitter and grouchy after that happened. Marnie was just relieved that she'd figured it out before accusing Lizette or Dane of anything.

"So what did Sawyer have to say for himself?" Marnie asked, exhaling for the first time in what seemed like eons.

"Nothing worth repeating." Lizette reached into her thin canvas messenger bag and brought out her cell phone. "Whatever. He's *so* hanging on by a thread."

Marnie's brow furrowed. She never thought Lizette would give up on her steaming-hot romance with Sawyer this quickly, especially because he was one of the most sought-after guys in their class.

This new boy must be an amazing catch.

"I don't know. I just feel like Sawyer is a total low-baller. I deserve someone way better than him," Lizette explained as she toyed with her phone.

"Really?" Marnie found that statement very hard to believe.

"I'm going to pee. Be right back," Lizette said as she put her phone down on the table and scampered off toward the rear of the coffeehouse.

Marnie leaned back on the couch and watched as a college-age girl with red hair began tuning her guitar onstage. Marnie was grateful that she and Lizette had their own place to hang out. Unlike Stewart's or Hoe

Bowl or a half-dozen other places in Poughkeepsie, there were no memories of Nola James lurking in the corners of the room, waiting to take hold of Marnie and wrestle her to the ground. However, her moment of tranquillity was disturbed when Lizette's phone broke into a Ludacris song.

When her eyes glanced at the caller ID and she saw Dane's name, Marnie almost crumbled to pieces.

So much for my payback theory.

Although Marnie had been thinking about messing around with Sawyer lately, she would never *act* on any of it. But once Dane's call went to Lizette's voice mail, Marnie couldn't ignore the facts. Something was going on between her kinda-sorta boyfriend and her new best friend, and she had to find out what.

The only question remaining was how.

Chapter 7

Homeroom was the last place Nola wanted to be on Wednesday morning. She hadn't seen or heard from Matt since he took off to meet his dad on Monday and he wasn't at his desk now, either. Nola anxiously fidgeted with the edge of her white fabric belt while contemplating several disastrous scenarios that would prevent Matt from coming to school or contacting her over the last forty-eight hours. Perhaps his father was in trouble with a loan shark, and Matt had to pawn all their belongings and move to the YMCA to save his dad from being capped. Or maybe Matt had to drive his father cross-country in order to donate bone marrow to one of their sick relatives. That was entirely in the realm of possibility!

Now if only Matt would call her and say he was on his way back home, Nola would stop worrying long enough to focus her energy on other important matters, like getting even with Marnie. Thanks to the Matt drama, Nola had lost her concentration over the last couple of days. But now that she glanced over at the almighty Lizette Levin, who was wearing the most ridiculous outfit today — baggy farmer overalls cuffed up to her knees over a chiffon peasant blouse — Nola's thirst for sweet revenge was instantaneously renewed.

"Attention, fellow classmates," boomed a cheery voice over the loudspeaker. *"Don't forget that the Poughkeepsie Central High School Homecoming weekend is October twenty-sixth and twenty-seventh. The big game against Iona Prep is on Friday night and the semiformal dance is on Saturday. Please see your student council representatives for tickets."*

Nola rolled her eyes as the chatter around her grew from a whisper to a loud roar. Everyone was in such a frenzy over Homecoming. Even scatterbrained spinster Miss Lucas appeared exuberant once she heard the words "semiformal dance." In fact, Nola's teacher grabbed her decrepit satchel and ran off to the ladies' room to "powder her nose," as if she was hoping to get lucky with one of the shop teachers during first period.

Stranger things have happened.

"So do *you* have a date to the dance yet, Nola?"

Nola glanced up to find Lizette looming over her like a giant milkmaid-mechanic. All of a sudden Nola's left leg began bobbing up and down like a buoy in the Hudson River, and her knuckles, of all things, started to itch. Lizette and Nola hadn't squared off since Deirdre's party, but she hadn't prepped herself for a catfight. Now that there was no Matt or Miss Lucas to intervene, she felt like a sitting duck. Still, Nola knew she couldn't ignore Lizette — she'd seen a show on the Discovery Channel once where a swimmer fought off a shark by punching it in the nose, and this situation seemed eerily similar.

"I'm sifting through an avalanche of offers, thanks for asking," Nola replied as she mustered up a small sneer.

Please go away now. Please, please, PLEASE!

Lizette put her hands on her hips and smirked impishly. "Ha! We all know you're going to stay at home and Bedazzle your Levi's while the rest of us are out partying."

Nola winced as she heard the sound of snickering echo throughout the room. Nola knew that she probably wasn't going to get asked to the Homecoming dance, by Matt or anyone else for that matter. But she hadn't really thought about the possibility of Matt going to the dance, dressing up in a suit, and wrapping Riley in his all-too-wonderful arms while a DJ spun "Weak" by JoJo. Right now it was *all* she could think about.

"Marnie and I are going to double, too," Lizette said haughtily. "We might even rent one of those stretch SUVs."

A vision of Marnie swapping spit with Dane while dressed in a vintage gown made Nola want to hurl all over Lizette's stupid Egyptian flat sandals.

"Why don't you give it a rest, Zee?"

The voice came from the row of desks near the window. Nola turned around and locked eyes with spiky-haired Sawyer Lee, who was mindlessly rolling the wheels on his skateboard with his hand. She gave him an appreciative smile and he grinned back.

Surprisingly, that was all Lizette needed to hear. After Sawyer spoke up, she just rolled her eyes, mumbled "What*ever*" under her breath, and retreated to her pack near Grier.

Nola heaved a sigh of relief when Lizette backed off. But when she filed into English class an hour and a half later and saw Marnie cheerily gabbing with Lizette outside the classroom door, Nola became so angry that she was literally seeing red. A crimson shade fell over everything in her path as if she had night-vision goggles on.

Nola rubbed at her eyes a few times and when she opened them, her eyesight had returned to normal. Even so, Nola was still furious at Lizette for embarrassing her in homeroom just for kicks and giggles, and pissed at Marnie for a litany of terrible things.

After the bell rang and latecomers, including Marnie, filed into the room, Mr. Quinn cleared his throat dramatically and instructed the class to read quietly from their textbooks while he caught up on grading their last vocabulary quiz. Nola took this as a chance to apologize (gag) to Marnie for yesterday and convince her to meet after school tonight to work on their school project. It was a stretch, true. But Nola thought that if she appealed to certain insecure parts of Marnie's personality that she knew like the back of her hand, she just might have some success.

Nola reached into her bag so that she could fish out her cell phone, but grunted in frustration when she realized that she'd left it on the charger at home. She'd have to resort to an old-school communication technique known as note passing. Nola hastily scribbled on a sheet of loose-leaf — *Sorry about the T.J. Maxx thing. It was uncalled for. We need to talk. About us and the group project. It's important.* — and folded it up into a small triangle. She leaned over in her chair, being careful not to make any noise and draw attention to herself, and tossed it onto Marnie's open textbook.

Marnie glanced over her shoulder and gave Nola a nasty sneer followed by an exaggerated eye roll. Even so, Marnie opened up the note and read it. Nola tapped her pencil nervously on the edge of her desk, which made Mr. Quinn cough in disapproval. She decided to sit on her hands while Marnie scrawled out a response. A few seconds later, the note landed on the floor near Nola's feet. She bent over in her chair and retrieved it, quickly unfolding it underneath her desk.

One minute. After class. That's it.

Nola crumpled up the piece of paper in her hand and glared at the back of Marnie's head. She was putting a *time limit* on their conversation now? What a control freak! If there was a slight chance of Nola backing down, Marnie had just killed it with one bullet to the head.

The rest of the class ebbed by so slowly that Nola swore she could feel gray hairs popping out of her scalp. She tried to keep busy by going over her spiel repeatedly in her head and telling herself not to lose her cool, no matter what Marnie did or said. Once the bell rang, Nola found herself in the exact same position as she had yesterday — standing a few feet away from her ex-best friend and about to launch a secret offensive attack.

Marnie's stance was poised but rigid as she readjusted her jean skirt on her hips. "What do you want, Nola?"

The harsh tone of Marnie's voice made Nola's ears hot. "Well, I really want to get an A on our oral report, and considering that you and I did that amazing presentation on the Sioux Indians last year, I figured —"

"Figured what?" Marnie said tersely.

"If you'd let me *finish,* I'd tell you," Nola said through gritted teeth.

Marnie sighed. "Fine."

"I figured you and I should meet on our own tonight so I can help you get the whole project organized. Sally and Evan are okay, but it's pretty clear that *you're* the only one who can make sure we ace this."

Good, appeal to Marnie's superiority complex!

"Wait a sec, *you* want to put *me* in charge?" Marnie raised one eyebrow skeptically and her tone remained icy.

"Who else?" Nola said. "You're the smartest one in the class."

Suddenly, Marnie's demeanor softened and she cracked somewhat of a smile.

Yes! It's working!

"What about . . . us, though?"

"Why don't we call a temporary, have-to-for-school-related cease-fire?" Nola suggested. "After our presentation, we don't have to say another word to each other again."

Even though Nola was acting out an award-winning performance, she felt a very real pain her chest when she heard herself say those words.

"I guess so," Marnie said.

Nola shifted her backpack from one shoulder to the other. "Want to meet up at Stewart's at around seven, then?"

It was a bold move, especially considering how many

of their memories lived on at that ice-cream parlor. But regardless of the sentiment Nola's suggestion had implied, Marnie nodded her head in agreement, packed up her belongings, and left for her next class.

Nola watched Marnie amble down the hall without a care in the world. But for once, Nola knew something that Marnie didn't know — that in hours, her ex-best friend would be at Stewart's, getting her just deserts.

Chapter 8

HOW TO AVOID DOING BODILY HARM TO NOLA FOR
THE SAKE OF MY ENGLISH GRADE
1) I'm stumped.

As Marnie sat at her kitchen table, sifting through her Helen Keller notes while finishing off her third piece of DiGiorno pizza, she thought back to earlier today when she agreed to spend the evening with Nola at their old hangout. Had she been sniffing glue or huffing paint at the time? Marnie searched her memory bank but she couldn't find anything out of the ordinary. It was puzzling. Why on earth had Marnie sunk so low as to even *talk* to Nola, let alone meet her at Stewart's?

Marnie popped a piece of crust in her mouth and put some papers in a green folder, including her most recent English quiz, which had a big bright red *F* written on the top. *Okay, maybe that's why.* Marnie's fingertips went numb just thinking about how she'd flunked the quiz because she had been too busy text-sparring with Nola. Marnie knew that she needed to do well on her group project or her mom might restrict her chill time with Lizette. That would suck out loud and in several different languages.

"Didn't you hear the doorbell?" Marnie's mom tugged on one of her small silver hoop earrings as she strolled through the kitchen.

Marnie frantically closed the folder and put it underneath her copy of *The Miracle Worker.* "Sorry, I guess I didn't."

Mrs. Fitzpatrick put a slice of pizza in the microwave and smiled. "Well, you have a visitor on the front porch. A very cute boy."

Marnie's stomach twisted into a tricky Boy Scout knot. A very cute boy could only be one person: Dane Harris. Under other circumstances, Marnie would have been bouncing off the walls, but instead she was anxious. While she loved the idea that Dane had stopped by to see her, she still couldn't help but wonder about his level of devotion. If he only had eyes for Marnie, why would he be chatting up Lizette on the side?

Mrs. Fitzpatrick walked over to Marnie, took her by the hands, and pulled her out of her chair. "Don't keep him waiting out there, or he'll leave before you get the chance to flirt with him."

"Gee, thanks for the advice, Mom," Marnie said as her mother dragged her to the door.

"Anytime." Mrs. Fitzpatrick kissed Marnie on the top of her head and then returned to the kitchen.

Even though Marnie had been a little disillusioned

about Dane as of late, she didn't think it was a reason to come to the door looking disheveled. She straightened out her denim skirt from H&M and adjusted her bra so that her yellow long-sleeve T-shirt from American Apparel was snug in all the right places. (Marnie had to admit, she was pleased with how she was looking tonight — Nola and her whack T.J.Maxx comments be damned!)

When Marnie opened the door, she was expecting to see Dane Harris's bright blue eyes staring back at her, but instead she was met with the pitch-black, midnight eyes of Sawyer Lee.

"I hope I'm not intruding." Sawyer held his colorful skateboard in his right hand as he yanked up his baggy parachute pants with the other.

Marnie saw a speck of skin near his hips and almost died. "Of course you're not."

"I just thought, maybe, you might want to . . . go for a walk or something," Sawyer said bashfully.

Marnie grinned at how nervous Sawyer was acting around her. How unbelievably adorable!

"Sure. I was actually heading over to Stewart's to meet —" Marnie paused, contemplating whether or not she should mention Nola. Sawyer might tell Lizette. Then once Lizette popped into her brain, Marnie's heart caved in like underdone soufflé. Even if Sawyer was on her porch, asking her to take a walk with him, nothing was going to come of it. On the other hand, what if Lizette and Dane were macking with each other behind her back?

"A friend." Marnie finally finished her sentence.

"Ah, you're a woman of mystery," Sawyer said, winking.

Marnie tried, but couldn't hold back a wide smile. "Just let me get my stuff."

After dashing to her room and grabbing her tote bag, Marnie bolted out the door with a clipped "good-bye-be-back-before-ten" to her mother. Then she slowed down her pace so that she wouldn't seem so eager to spend time with Sawyer.

As Sawyer coasted along the sidewalk on his skate-board, Marnie kept up to speed with him, thankful that she'd put on the pair of breathable Geox sneakers she'd bought on eBay early in the summer. There was nothing but silence between them for the first block or two, but when they hit a blinking DON'T WALK sign, Marnie decided she might as well find out why Sawyer had stopped by to begin with.

Marnie clutched at her bag and hoped that she didn't scare Sawyer off. "So how did you find out where I live?"

Yep, you practically accused him of stalking you, Marn. Way to go!

Sawyer half grinned and stepped off his skateboard, kicking the back of it with his right foot so the front end leaped up and catching it with one of his hands.

That was so hawt*!*

"On a scale of one to ten — one being the least creepiest thing anyone has ever said to you, and ten being the most creepiest thing — how does 'I asked Chang from the Chinese restaurant' strike you as a response?"

Marnie bit her lower lip to stop herself from breaking out into the girliest giggle known to humankind. "I'd give it a four."

"That's not too bad," Sawyer replied, nodding at the sign that was now blinking WALK. "Ladies first."

Marnie sashayed across the street with the confidence of a hundred Erin Fitzpatricks. Sawyer had gone through *that* much trouble to track her down! There was definitely more to this "walk" than met the eye.

As they came to the corner, Sawyer stopped Marnie right in her path and put his skateboard down in front of her feet.

"Want to give it a try?" he asked.

Marnie briefly flashed back to five years ago when she'd almost broken her neck on Nola's Dora the Explorer three-wheeled scooter as she tried to perform some daring stunt. "No, that's okay," she said warily.

Sawyer flashed a megawatt smile as he laughed. "Are you afraid or something?"

"Oh, please," Marnie said as she walked around him, swinging her hips a little more than usual.

Sawyer darted ahead of her and then blocked her way once again. "I triple-dog dare you."

Marnie tossed her head and whipped her wavy blonde hair when she laughed. "That line may work on Brian Bennington, but it won't on me."

She tried to take a step forward but Sawyer closed in to the point where they were almost touching chest to chest. "What if I held your hand? Would that help?"

"It might," Marnie said breathlessly.

Sawyer backed up a few feet and placed the skateboard on the ground. "I won't let you fall, Marnie," he said, holding his hand out for her to take.

Marnie swallowed hard and reached out for Sawyer's fingerless-gloved hand. When she felt it squeeze hers tightly, she almost trembled.

Sawyer put Marnie's bag on his shoulder and kept her steady as she hopped on his skateboard, but she shrieked a bit when the wheels began to shift back and forth. Marnie covered her eyes with her other hand in embarrassment, but then started to laugh when Sawyer snickered.

"Quit it, you'll make me lose my concentration," Marnie chided him jokingly.

"But we're not even *moving* yet," Sawyer replied.

"I know! That's why you should stop messing around," Marnie said, remembering all too well how much it hurt when she flew off that three-wheeled scooter into Nola's next-door neighbor's rosebush.

A serious look came over Sawyer's sun-kissed face. "You're right. I'm sorry."

"Okay, then. Let's start off *slowly*."

"You bet. Slow as a turtle."

Marnie's heart began to quiver as Sawyer tugged her along by the hand and the skateboard picked up some speed. "Make that a *tortoise!*"

Instead, Sawyer increased the pace and began to jog, dragging her along behind him. "We'll never make it to Stewart's at that rate, Marnie. Just hold on tight!"

"I'm in no rush!" Marnie's voice was trembling a bit. But then she felt him give her hand an affectionate squeeze and her fears fluttered away. In fact, Marnie saw the houses flying by and the sidewalk whizzing underneath the skateboard and a familiar rush of adrenaline overcame her — only it wasn't the kind she felt on her morning runs.

It was more like how Marnie felt when she'd first kissed Dane Harris. But better.

Marnie's magical skateboard ride came to an end two blocks before Stewart's, much to her disappointment. She could have held on to Sawyer's hand and glided around her neighborhood for hours. But no, she had to work on her English group project with *Nola*. Being civil to her ex-best friend for longer than a fraction of a second was definitely going to test her patience and sanity.

However, as Marnie stood and stared at the colorful awning in the not-so-far distance, a thousand different happy memories came flooding back to her, like the time she and Nola tried to stuff themselves full of root beer floats or when Marnie flung a cherry at Nola's head and they got into a mini-hot-fudge-sundae fight. When she reflected on all the drama she was dealing with now — her growing feelings for Sawyer, Lizette possibly hooking up with Dane on the DL, and Brynne acting like the crazy, just-out-of-rehab version of Courtney Love — Marnie couldn't help but feel that if Nola was in her life like she used to be, everything would make sense.

"Quarter for your thoughts," Sawyer said, tugging at Marnie's shirtsleeve.

Marnie kept her sights trained on the road ahead of her. She was scared of gazing into Sawyer's hypnotizing dark eyes and what might happen next if she did.

"Aren't you supposed to be offering me a penny?" she asked.

"Well, I think you're worth more than that."

Oh, my God, that's hella *sweet!*

Marnie spun around to face him, and lo and behold, his mesmerizing eyes were pulling her in like an isotope magnet.

"Are you nervous about meeting your 'friend'?" From the smirk on Sawyer's face and the air quotes he made with his fingers, Marnie could see that he assumed she was having a secret rendezvous with a boy other than Dane. Which was ironic, considering the chemistry between her and Sawyer right now. Still, Marnie wasn't about to let Sawyer get the wrong idea. She wasn't the cheating type.

At least not yet.

"I am nervous, actually. We're in a big fight and we haven't hung out with each other since," Marnie explained.

"Is this Nola we're talking about?"

For some reason, Marnie now wasn't worried about Sawyer telling Lizette that she had met up with Nola. In fact, she felt as though whatever she told Sawyer would stay between the two of them, which was ridiculous, really. Sawyer and Lizette were a bona fide couple, and she and Sawyer were just . . . completely undefined.

"Yeah, it is," Marnie admitted.

"Zee has it in for that girl." Sawyer reached into his pocket and checked his cigarette stash. "You should have seen the way she was taunting Nola in homeroom this morning."

"Really?" Marnie said in disbelief.

"Yep, it was brutal," Sawyer said as he took out a cigarette and put it between his lips. "Actually, it just added to all the doubts I have about Zee. On the one hand, she's smart and pretty and funny. On the other hand, she has this mean streak."

Marnie remembered how cruelly Lizette had treated her at the football game when she had seen Marnie and Sawyer goofing around together, and how Lizette had sold Marnie out to Brynne by revealing private jokes. Up until now, Marnie hadn't attributed those things to Lizette's having a mean streak, but she was suddenly reluctant to defend Lizette and dismiss Sawyer's comments.

"Anyway, that's why I've been lying real low." Sawyer took out a book of matches and lit his cigarette, then inhaled a long drag and blew out a puff of smoke along with a frustrated sigh. "I probably shouldn't be telling you this. You two are tight."

"It's okay, my lips are sealed." Marnie was stunned by Sawyer's catharsis. Not only had he described exactly what *she'd* been feeling about Lizette lately, but he'd also trusted Marnie enough to tell her about the shaky state of his relationship.

"As far as Nola goes," he went on, "just follow your gut instinct. It'll never steer you wrong."

Sawyer tossed his cigarette on the ground and smothered it with the sole of his shoe. Then he hopped on his skateboard and grinned at her. "I know how girly this sounds, but thanks for taking a walk with me. I really needed someone to vent to."

Marnie giggled as she tossed her blonde hair over her shoulder. "Anytime."

Before Sawyer rolled off, he gave Marnie a silly military salute and said, "Fare thee well." But as Marnie approached the front door of Stewart's, she was not faring well at all.

Chapter 9

After eating three scoops of ice cream (pistachio, strawberry, and butter pecan — each of them served on its own small sugar cone), Nola was feeling very sick to her stomach. She wouldn't have oinked out like this if Weston Briggs had been on time to meet her at Stewart's — she'd told him to be here at six-thirty *on the dot*. Didn't punctuality mean anything to him? Then again, Weston only cared about two things — baseball and himself. Considering that it was play-off season, she was lucky that Weston had agreed to leave his living room and big-screen TV for ten minutes.

Nola put her hands on her belly in an attempt to calm her queasiness, but she could still feel it grumbling. She hadn't been this nauseous from ice cream since the summer of seventh grade. Nola and Marnie had been obsessed with the *Guinness Book of World Records* and decided that their only way into the ranks was to drink their weight in root beer floats in less than forty-eight hours. Marnie outlasted Nola, of course — Marnie had been living off junk food for years so her internal organs were conditioned for this kind of eating challenge — but Nola's body went into some type of dairy shock after forcing her fifth float down her throat.

However, as Nola leaned back in her chair and drank some tepid water with a slice of lemon, she told herself that after today, everything would be different. She would no longer be the shy girl who couldn't stand up for herself, or the wimpy girl who'd rather scratch her hives instead of face her fears. Nola James 2.0 was a kick-ass-and-take-names kind of girl, and in a short while, she'd make her debut, courtesy of a ghost from Marnie's past.

Yet if the ghost didn't show up soon, Nola would be forced to perform an emergency séance in the middle of an ice-cream shop.

Nola turned her head toward the door when she heard the sound of tiny bells jingling, but she sighed heavily when she saw that the boy who walked in was just Jeremy Atwood. Nola watched him approach the counter and park himself on a stool. It was a tad strange to hear the waitress ask Jeremy, "You want the usual?" Nola thought she and Marnie were the only regular customers at Stewart's who had signature orders. But when Nola's mind flashed back to the Saturday afternoon she and Matt had shared a sundae, she remembered spotting Jeremy perched on the same stool, eating the same exact thing — a double scoop of rocky road in a dish. Nola felt a little sorry for him, though. She couldn't recall seeing Jeremy here with anyone else. Although

Nola had lost her best friend recently, thankfully she hadn't endured the sad experience of eating ice cream all by her lonesome.

The bells jingled again, but this time, Weston pushed open the front door and sauntered over to Nola's table, bending the brim of his Red Sox hat so that his sparkling eyes were barely visible. Then he slumped down in the seat across from Nola and cracked his knuckles loudly.

"What's up?" he asked while jutting out his perfectly dimpled chin.

"You were supposed to be here at six-thirty." Nola zipped up the front of her Theory cable-knit fisherman's sweater right up to her collarbone.

"In case you didn't know, there's a pennant race going on," Weston said snidely. "Be happy that I came at all."

Nola swallowed hard. She had to remind him why he was here or else risk losing him altogether. "Isn't seeing Marnie more important? She's *really* been looking forward to this."

Weston stretched his well-toned arms above his head and smirked. "I bet she has."

Ugh. Could this guy be any more full of himself?

Even though she was quite disgusted with Weston at the moment, Nola knew stroking his ego was the best way to keep him from rushing to the nearest house with a satellite dish and an ESPN channel package.

"Well, I'm not surprised, either. She hasn't stopped talking about you since you broke up," Nola said with conviction. "Don't tell her I told you this, but she still looks at pics of you on her camera phone."

Weston smiled so widely, Nola was wondering if he'd caught his reflection in someone's spoon. "So where is she, then?" he asked.

Nola checked her watch. T-minus ten minutes and counting. All she had to do was pull the wool over Weston's eyes (which shouldn't be too hard — Marnie had told her he was held back in the second grade) and then let it all play out from the other side of the front window.

"She's en route," Nola said. "I'm going to make myself scarce in a bit so that you two lovebirds can be alone. But here's the thing. Marnie's going to act like she's not expecting to see you."

The corners of Weston's mouth curled up. "Why would she do that?"

Nola was so nervous about this next prong in the plan that she was wringing her hands underneath the table. She'd rehearsed her lines a hundred times in her head and it was crucial that she didn't flub them.

Okay, take a deep cleansing breath and . . . DON'T SCREW THIS UP!

"Marnie developed this rare . . . sleepwalking disorder since you've been gone."

"Sleepwalking disorder?" The tone of Weston's voice was definitely skeptical.

Nola could feel a hive popping up on her neck and wished that she could zip her sweater up over her head. "Yeah. She was in all the medical journals last month. It was pretty cool."

"Well, why would she be sleepwalking *now*? It's dinnertime."

Good point.

"Weston, Weston, Weston," Nola said, trying to stall and think of a reasonable explanation. She nervously tore up a napkin as she waited for a brilliant idea to strike, and thankfully one did. "Don't you remember how Marnie loved . . . *naps*?

You got 'em, Nol. Who doesn't *love naps?*

Weston scratched at his ear with a bandaged finger and squinted. "Uh, I think so."

Woo-hoo! He's putty in your hands!

"Anyway, just don't sweat it if she's acting weird. It's only Mr. Sandman talking. Deep down, she's infatuated with you, and that's what counts." Nola was in total awe of herself. The lies were piling up so fast, but she hadn't cracked under the pressure.

"Whatever you say, Nola," Weston replied as he pulled out his Samsung BlackJack phone and began checking baseball scores.

Nola smiled with pride. She had somehow managed to con Weston *and* Marnie in the same day! Who knew that she could be so shrewd? Obviously no one, which was probably why Nola's falsehoods were flying under the radar. Marnie and Weston would never suspect innocent, naive little Nola could concoct a foolproof scheme such as this. And that was definitely the most satisfying thing about revenge.

It was equally sweet and vicious.

Chapter 10

Marnie's chat with Sawyer had left her all discombobu-
lated, both physically and mentally. With each step, her
legs felt as though they were trudging through a sand
dune, and the percentage of her brain that *wasn't* thinking about Sawyer's unparalleled hotness was about to
combust. When she finally pushed open the door at
Stewart's, Marnie had almost forgotten why she was
there.

Oh, yeah, homework with Nola. The ultimate buzz-kill.

Marnie heaved a resigned sigh, put her hands on her
hips, and quickly scanned the room for Nola's mopey
face. All the tables but one were filled, but Nola wasn't
at any of them. Marnie pulled out her pink Razr phone
from her tote and checked the time. She had made it
with minutes to spare, but apparently Nola had gotten
held up, so Marnie made a beeline for the empty table
and sat down.

After a minute or two went by, Marnie thought
about ordering a double scoop ice-cream cone to go and
heading home, but realized that was a bit too hasty.
Even though Nola was Marnie's *ex*-best friend, she
deserved some courtesy. However, when five more minutes passed, Marnie started to reconsider. How hard

was it for Nola to call and say she was going to be late? Didn't she think Marnie had anything better to do than wait around for her to show up for a project meeting that *she* had suggested to begin with?

Another minute ticked by, and Marnie was growing furious. She dug back into her tote and nabbed her phone, flipping it open so she could scroll through the contacts and select Nola's name. It wasn't until she came to her mom's best friend, Nancy, that she remembered deleting Nola's number during English class a few days before. Marnie stared at the screen on her phone and wondered if Nola had done the same thing, and that's why she hadn't called.

Marnie shook her head in bewilderment. How could two people who had known each other for eight years be completely incommunicado because they deleted each other's info from their cell phones? If they were really best friends, wouldn't they know each other's numbers by heart? They certainly knew everything else.

"Are you looking at pictures of me again?" a familiar voice said from no more than three feet away.

When Marnie glanced up and saw the wicked grin on Weston Briggs's drop-dead gorgeous face, she accidentally bit the side of her tongue.

What the hell is HE doing here?

"It's good to see you, Marnie," Weston said as he straightened his baseball cap and smirked. "Aren't you going to invite me to sit down?"

Marnie was pretty sure her tongue was bleeding and that she'd eventually need medical attention once she gouged out her eyes, which would most likely happen in the next four to seven seconds. Looking at Weston — the infamous ex-boyfriend she had *just* gotten over this summer — and his perfect nose, ears, mouth, chin, shoulders, chest, legs, and hair was enough to make Marnie wish for Greek tragedy–style death.

Only one person knew how weak she could be when it came to Weston, and that was Nola. But Nola wasn't here to protect her, and even if she were, there was a good chance she'd turn her back on Marnie and walk the other way. Marnie was undoubtedly on her own.

Now if she could just snap herself out of the shock of seeing her ex-boyfriend, she might be able to say something — anything!

"I can tell that you're happy to see me, too." Weston grabbed hold of the chair across from Marnie with his large hands, twirled it around, and plopped down on it. "You look . . . amazing."

Marnie managed a half grin. Although she was about to hurl all over her Geox, she was delighted that Weston thought she was hot. But the delight was short-lived once Marnie remembered the last thing Weston had ever said to her. It was right before he dropped the bomb that he was moving to Arizona and would probably never see Marnie again.

We had a good run, Marn, but our time has come to an end. I've got to take this team on the road and put someone else in my starting lineup.

Yes, the guy Marnie had thought was her soul mate had used a tired and clichéd baseball metaphor to break up with her.

Was there anything more humiliating than that?

Marnie hadn't believed so, until this moment was upon her.

"I don't think *happy* is the right adjective," she said, snapping her phone shut forcefully.

Weston stretched his arms in front of him and checked out his triceps. "You're right. *Thrilled* is probably more like it."

Oh, puh-lease! Like I even give two craps now!

"What are you doing back in Poughkeepsie, anyway?" Marnie tried to avert her eyes so she wouldn't stare at the adorable birthmark on Weston's chin.

"My dad got his job back at Marist, so I'm here to stay," he explained.

Great, just great.

Weston leaned forward and ran his finger down

Marnie's arm. "So are we going to get out of here or what?"

Marnie reclined so far back in her chair, it was about to tip over. "Or what."

"I'd forgotten how cute you are," Weston said, laughing. "Let's just skip the small talk and head for the shed behind your house, like the old days. I *know* you want to."

Marnie gasped. They hadn't spoken in almost a year and now he shows up out of the blue, wanting a spontaneous shed hook-up? Had someone hit him in the head with a wooden bat recently?

"I'm sorry but you must have me confused with the girl in your starting lineup," she snapped. "I don't want to go *anywhere* with you."

Weston chuckled again, clearly amused by Marnie's ire. "Nola said you might act like you weren't expecting me."

Marnie's brow furrowed in confusion.

Nola told him what?

Suddenly, Weston began clapping his hands in front of Marnie's face.

"What the hell are you doing?" she asked crossly.

"I'm trying to wake you up," Weston said, still clapping away. "Nola said this would work if you were sleepwalking."

Marnie's body temperature immediately rose from normal to the environmental temperature on Mars. Nola had never intended to work on their English project together. She had set up this whole embarrassing scenario with Weston from the beginning, and Marnie walked right into her trap like a dumb (but supercute) bunny.

But now that Marnie was onto Nola, all of her senses were heightened. So much so, she could feel someone staring at her from behind — the same feeling she'd experienced during English class.

Marnie turned around and saw Nola gaping at her from outside Stewart's front window. However, instead of running away once she realized Marnie had spotted her, Nola stood her ground, glaring at Marnie like she wanted to rumble.

However, instead of facing her bitter enemy, a teary-eyed Marnie went into a full retreat and hid out in the ladies' room, asking herself over and over again how the shy, meek Nola James had gotten the better of her.

She never came up with an answer.

Chapter 11

Nola scrambled home from Stewart's in ten minutes flat. She'd never made that kind of time before, not even when she had been chased by water gun–toting Dennis and Dylan at the end of July. As she scurried along the sidewalks in her neighborhood, Nola felt carefree and almost elated. She had exacted revenge against someone who had hurt her badly, and witnessing Marnie run off to the bathroom in near hysterics had given Nola a sense of pride that she hadn't anticipated. When she arrived at the steps to her front porch, out of breath and sweating, Nola was still so keyed up she felt as though she could gallop all the way to Matt's house and back.

Nola sat on the bottom step and rested her head in her hands. She tried to regulate her shallow breathing by counting slowly from one to ten. About a minute later, Nola's chest rose and fell with ease, but regardless, doubtful thoughts began to seep into her mind. A small voice kept asking Nola if her actions were justified, and a strong-willed voice would always reply, "Um, *yeah!*"

The facts remained the facts. Marnie had instigated this whole thing, and if she hadn't been the traitor she was, Marnie would be sitting here on the stairs of Nola's house at dusk, not stuck in a trap laid by her ex-best friend's cunning ingenuity. A trap that Nola herself didn't think she could pull off. But she had — flawlessly, in fact!

Could I feel any better than I do right now?!

"Nice night, isn't it?"

Nola turned and looked over her shoulder, hoping that she had just imagined that deep, annoying voice. But she was wrong. Ian Capshaw was there, closing the door behind him and walking out onto the porch in his signature black Pumas. Although there was just a shred of moonlight surfacing from behind a small cluster of clouds, Nola couldn't help but notice how Ian's eyes glinted as he cast his gaze upward at the sound of a plane traveling over Poughkeepsie's city limits.

"I suppose," Nola replied, thinking how unbelievably not-so-nice she became when she was within spitting distance of the family manny.

Ian traipsed down the steps, brushed off a patch of wood next to Nola, and sat down. "Can't we agree on anything?" he asked playfully.

Nola smirked. "Maybe."

"That's not very encouraging." Ian pointed up to the jet stream that was floating in the air. "Do you think that fuel emissions contribute to the greenhouse effect?"

Nola shrugged her shoulders. "Yeah, it's possible."

"Great, we've found our common ground," Ian said with a grin. "Let's not deviate from environmental issues, okay?"

Nola chuckled again, but then quickly shot Ian a suspicious look. Why was he being so pleasant all of a sudden? He'd barely said a word to her after their confrontation the other day. Ian had to have an ulterior motive, *or* was planning on saying something obnoxious within the next millisecond. Either way, Nola wasn't sure she could rely on this unexpected burst of congeniality.

"So . . . where have you been?" Ian asked.

I knew it!

Nola sighed and shook her head. "I can't believe you're asking me this *again!*"

Ian put up his hands as if he was surrendering. "It's relevant to the environment, I swear!"

"Gimme a break, Ian." Nola stood up and stomped over to the porch swing, sitting down in a huff. "I may be a freshman in high school, but I'm not that gullible."

Ian stayed put on the stairs and shifted his position so that he was leaning back against the railing and stretching his legs out in front of him. "Honest, Nola. Your whereabouts are critical to the state of global warming because . . . because . . ." Ian paused for a moment, obviously searching for convincing words.

Nola grabbed the chains on either side of the swing, trotted back a bit, and then glided forward. "Oh, I can't wait to hear what's next."

"Why do you have to be so . . . combative? I'm just trying to look out for you." Ian picked up a stray piece of stone that was wedged in between two porch floor planks and chucked it onto the lawn.

Nola glanced at Ian and saw a pinkish tint form on his cheeks. It made her want to believe that he was being sincere, but she'd thought that before and gotten burned. Still, Nola decided to give him the benefit of the doubt, even though she had no idea why.

"I'm not *combative,*" she said as the swing continued to rock her back and forth. "I'm just not used to so much . . . attention. It makes me uncomfortable."

Ian brought his legs in so that he could prop his elbows up on his knees. "I really don't mean to be on your case. And I know I don't always say or do the perfect thing, but I hope eventually you will learn to trust me."

Nola flashed back to fifteen minutes earlier, when she was staring at Marnie through the window of Stewart's. After all the drama of the past few weeks, would she be able to trust anyone ever again, even herself?

*   *   *

At around ten-thirty, Nola came out of her shower, wrapped in a long blue terry-cloth robe that her grandmother had gotten her at Crabtree & Evelyn two Christmases ago. Ian had left for the night when her mom had returned from the hospital at nine, and her little brothers were tucked into their beds, at least for the time being — Dennis and Dylan were known for their late-night shenanigans, which usually included full-throttle pillow fights.

Nola toweled off her tangled honey brown hair and fingered in some Neutrogena Triple Moisture Leave-In Cream conditioner, making sure the split ends were saturated just as much as her roots. Once she started running a fine-tooth comb through her locks, Nola began to hear that doubtful voice again, questioning her ethics. But immediately, Nola realized that she was being too hard on herself. It wasn't like she was a vindictive person. Actually, she was the exact opposite! No one could deny that Nola had been a caring, sensitive, and loyal friend to Marnie. Not even a certain boy who had taken Marnie's place.

Only that same certain boy had disappeared without a trace again.

Nola flopped down on her desk chair and checked her e-mail. When she looked at her in-box, she had a new e-mail, but it wasn't from Matt. After the word *sender* was the name RILEY FINNEGAN.

Nola was so flabbergasted she almost fell off her chair.

Without hesitation, she double-clicked on the subjectless message.

to: *nolaj1994@gmail.com*
from: *rf@rileyfinneganswake.com*
date: *Wednesday, October 3, 10:24* P.M.

Hi, Nola!
How are you? I asked Matt for your e-mail addy when I got back to NJ. Hope you don't mind that he handed your deets over. ☺
 It sucks that we didn't get to hang more when I was in Po-town — I thought you were wicked cool though, especially when I found out that YOU MADE MY NECKLACE! I took a sweet pic of it yesterday with my cam phone and posted it on my blog so everyone could see. You should totally check it out.
 So, the reason I'm writing (curious, huh?). Matt has been acting kind of strange since I came to visit. Would you happen to know why? I mean, Matt tells me everything, of course. He even

mentioned how devastated he was when you thought he had messed with your friend's posters. (FYI: Matt was on the phone with me for hours that night because I had this Web site crisis, so it wasn't him.) Anyway, since you're Matt's friend, I figured you had behind-the-scenes info, because it seems like it's more than the typical stuff stressing him out. So if you do know something, I'd appreciate it if you could fill me in. It would be on the DL, promise.

Talk soon,

RF

Nola laughed out loud after she finished the e-mail. How could Riley be asking *her* of all people about why Matt was *acting strange?* Talk about ironic. Nola didn't even know where he was! Riley also had a lot of nerve to try and wring privileged information out of Matt's friends. If there was a referee around, he'd certainly call a foul on Riley for going behind Matt's back like this.

But what ticked off Nola the most was how Riley was pretending to care about her and the bracelet and hanging out more in "Po-town." The girl was so freaking false! She just wanted to sweet-talk Nola into giving up the goods on Matt, and there was no way Nola would ever do that, even if she did know what was wrong with him, beyond the "typical stuff." Besides, Riley had mentioned at the party that the police were somehow involved in Matt's life, and Nola didn't know a damn thing about that.

Maybe she should call the local sheriff and ask him why Matt is "acting strange"!

Nola was about to hit the DELETE button when something finally occurred to her. Riley had given Matt an alibi for the night when Marnie's posters had been wrecked. She'd also described Matt as being "devastated" when Nola thought he was involved somehow. Nola swallowed hard and rubbed the back of her neck, which was suddenly tight and stiff. Not only was Matt completely off the hook for being directly involved with vandalism, but Riley had also admitted that Matt was a total mess over *Nola.* And now he was acting strange, and Riley assumed Nola would know why.

Maybe Nola hadn't been kidding herself, and her luck was about to change. Could it be that Matt and Riley were on the rocks?

Nola's phone buzzed before she finished that train of thought. She reached over to the far end of her desk where her cell was plugged in to its charger and looked at the caller ID. Nola leaped off her chair and started jumping up and down as if she'd just won a GemMall

.com shopping spree, then took a deep breath and accepted the call.

"Hello?"

"Hey, Nol. Sorry to call so late."

It was so great to hear Matt's tender yet slightly gravelly voice. Especially now that Nola sensed that Riley was feeling insecure about their relationship.

"That's okay," she said softly. "Is everything all right? I haven't seen or heard from you in a while."

"Yeah, I know." Matt sounded heartbroken. "I'm out of town . . . with my dad."

Nola's head was filling with questions, but Matt's tone concerned her so much that she didn't want to bombard him with them. At the same time, she had a feeling that if she did press him, he'd run off again.

"I see," she said as she sat on the edge of her bed and peered down at her bare size eight-and-a-half feet.

"Look, I feel terrible about keeping things from you, Nol. You gotta know that." Frequent bouts of static were making Matt's words come out fuzzy, but Nola was hanging on each and every one. "But I'm kind of doing it to . . . protect us. I don't expect you to under-stand what that means right now, but you will, I promise."

A profound sigh came through clearly amid the

static. For some odd reason, Nola didn't care one bit if she ever understood why Matt was hiding from her. All Nola could think about was the one word she was still hanging on: *Us.*

"Will I see you in school tomorrow?"

"I'm not sure. My dad and I are still pretty tied up," Matt said, his volume rising in an attempt to battle the static.

Nola's eyes watered at the idea of not seeing Matt for another day.

God, I am PATHETIC!

"Do me a favor, though," Matt said.

"What?"

"Don't go running off with another guy while I'm away, got that?" he joked.

Nola wiped a tear from her right cheek as she laughed. That would never happen in a million years.

"I won't."

"Good," he replied.

Soon afterward, they said their good-byes, and Nola went to sleep, but she held on to Matt's voice until the sun came up.

Chapter 12

On Thursday morning, Marnie came to school dressed for hand-to-hand combat. She'd thrown on an outfit that would intimidate the Goth kids — Double-H black steel-toed cowboy boots over black leggings; a black, distressed-washed cutoff denim mini, and a black three-quarter-length-sleeve pullover with a glittery red pitchfork on the front, which she'd gotten at Hot Topic right after Weston Briggs broke up with her. When she came home last night, Marnie had made a pinkie-swear promise to herself that there would be no more retreating. In fact, now Marnie was going to live by one of the rules in Weston's precious playbook — the key to a good defense is a killer offense.

That being said, she planned on doing some serious damage to her lying, deceiving, all-around reprehensible opponent during English class. As far as Marnie was concerned, the gloves were not only off, but they were permanently banned from this full-contact sport.

"My, my, Marnie. Are you the freshman class treasurer or a Hell's Angel?" Lizette said snidely as she and Grier escorted Marnie to her locker after homeroom.

Marnie sized Lizette up from head to toe and chuckled. In other parts of the world, people might have thought it was ironic of Lizette to criticize someone else's fashion sense, considering she was wearing a red-and-white-checked jumper that could double as a restaurant tablecloth, a ginormous gold patent leather belt, and a pair of bright purple Crocs. But here at Poughkeepsie Central, no one doubted the haute couture authority of Lizette Levin.

Except for Marnie, that is. After what happened at Cubbyhole the other night, Marnie was plenty doubtful about Lizette. Still, she couldn't bring herself to either confront Lizette or engage in some Nancy Drew–style snooping like she'd originally intended. Now that Marnie had Nola, Brynne, *and* Weston nipping at her, she felt as though everyone was out for her blood. And despite the fact that there was a thin veil of suspicion over Lizette and Dane, she couldn't risk tipping the boat into barracuda-infested waters. Besides, all Dane was guilty of was calling Lizette on her cell phone. Sawyer made an impromptu visit to Marnie's house yesterday and she wasn't exactly blabbing to Lizette about it!

Actually, Marnie wasn't planning on mentioning it at all.

"This is my take-no-BS outfit," she said as she opened her locker door and checked her reflection in a small magnetic mirror. "I thought you'd like it."

Grier picked a piece of lint off Marnie's T-shirt. "It's *way* fierce, Marnie."

Lizette cracked her gum and rolled her eyes. "Um, Grier, that word is *so* passé. Now we say boss."

"Oh. Okay, Zee!" Grier chirped.

Marnie smirked. Leave it to Lizette to make a unilateral statement like that and have Grier agree without any discussion. Marnie was happy that she wasn't *that* much of a follower.

"Anyway, who's giving you BS?" Lizette asked.

"Ugh. It's Nola," Marnie said as she smoothed out her eyebrows and pinched her cheeks to give them a rosy hue.

"Oh, what*ever*," Lizette growled. "That girl is worthless. You're *so* much better off without her. So what'd she do to you?" Lizette added as she pushed Marnie to the side and inspected her eye makeup in Marnie's mirror.

"It's a long, twisted story. I'll have to save it for lunch," Marnie replied.

"*Ooooooh*. Sounds juicy," Grier cooed.

Lizette reapplied her black cherry–flavored Stila lip glaze. "Well, I'm eating with Sawyer today. I've decided to give him one more chance to prove himself before I cut him loose and pursue . . . other options."

Marnie swallowed hard. Not only was she suddenly

feeling a little guilty about her afternoon skateboard tryst with Sawyer, but she was also dreading having lunch with the spawn of Satan, a.k.a. Brynne. Although Grier meant well, she wasn't a great buffer and would probably wail herself into a stupor if Brynne and Marnie bared their claws.

"I guess I'll text you about it during first period then."

"Coolio," Lizette said. "I'll help you backhand her, Marn, don't worry."

"Thanks, Zee." Marnie reached up to grab her textbooks for her first two classes when two hands came up from behind and tickled her sides. She yelped in surprise and turned to find herself boots-to-loafers with Dane.

"Hey, pretty girl." He touched the tip of Marnie's nose with his finger and smiled brilliantly.

Marnie *really* wanted to act aloof. But when she smelled Dane's Yves Saint Laurent cologne, the word *aloof* evaporated from her vocabulary quicker than *cease-fire*.

"Hey," Marnie said with a sexy grin. "What are you doing in freshman hall?"

Lizette began putting her blonde hair up in a bun, which made her jumper creep up so high it could be considered indecent exposure in some of the more liberal Midwestern states. Marnie caught Dane checking out Lizette's legs, but Marnie couldn't blame him because she and Grier were, too.

"Looking for trouble, aren't you, Dane?" Lizette said lightheartedly.

"Well, since you're here, Zee, I suppose I've found it," Dane joked.

Lizette threw her head back and guffawed.

Oh, will they knock it off already?!

As her face turned crimson, Marnie spun around and stood on her tiptoes, reaching for the textbooks on the top shelf of her locker. Dane leaned over her gallantly and snatched them for her.

"I came by to ask you out for Friday night," he said, gripping Marnie's books with his large and impeccably clean hands. "Are you free?"

For a brief moment, Marnie remembered how cozy Lizette and Dane were at the coffeehouse and how sweaty Sawyer's hands were when she was racing down the street on his skateboard and she almost told Dane no. But instead, Marnie shook those memories out of her head and said, "Yes, I am."

"Great," Dane said with a seductive wink. "I have a surprise for you."

When the first bell rang, students everywhere scattered left and right as Marnie, Lizette, and Dane ambled along at their own pace, like the rule-makers they were. But when Marnie and Grier strolled in the direction of their first-period classroom while Lizette and Dane walked off together, laughing as though they were sharing a secret, Marnie realized she'd had enough surprises.

An hour later, Marnie was sitting in English class, waiting anxiously for Mr. Quinn to ask his students to get into their groups. Oral reports were to be presented next Thursday and counted for a third of their first-quarter grades. Even though Marnie had been stressing about her recent F yesterday, she wasn't fixated on what letter would end up in the English column of her report card at the moment. She was too preoccupied with much, *much* more important matters, like slamming Nola James so hard that the aftershock would be felt throughout all of upstate New York and some parts of Canada, too.

Marnie slowly craned her neck so that she could steal a quick peek at her rival but was stunned when she saw Nola sneering at her already. Marnie had hoped that they would lock eyes so she could cut Nola down to size with a razor-sharp glare, but Nola had already beaten her to it. Marnie hadn't thought that Nola's boldness would last. The Nola James she used to be friends with was timid and kind of spineless, and after her powwow with Lizette this morning, Marnie was convinced that Nola really *was* worthless. However, from the way Nola was scowling at her, it appeared that the feeling was mutual.

"Okay, folks. You have a few minutes to meet in your groups," Mr. Quinn announced as he gripped the lapels of his dark blue wool blazer. "And if I catch any of you playing with your cell phones or those Webkinz things, I'll confiscate them. I mean it!"

Everyone began moving their seats into small clusters while Mr. Quinn searched for the sports section in the mess of papers that was on his desk. Marnie picked up her things and moved to a desk at the front left corner of the room while perky Sally Applebaum and geeky Evan Sanders followed along. Marnie clenched her fists and straightened her posture as a composed, audacious-looking Nola headed straight for her.

Think offense, Marnie. Tough, New England Patriots–style offense!

Marnie recalled all the texts Lizette had sent her during first period and prepped herself for her act of vindication. She had to hand it to Lizette — even though the quality of her character had been in question as of late, she really came through for Marnie when she needed it. And in a moment, Lizette's brilliant scheme would be carried out to perfection by Marnie.

"So Nola, did you manage to get that Braille book we talked about last week?" Sally asked as Nola took a seat next to her.

Marnie watched Nola cross her arms over her chest tightly, a move that unnerved Marnie more than it ought to.

"I've been busy," Nola said with a snide smile that belonged on the likes of wenches like Brynne Callaway.

Marnie felt an anxious fluttering in her stomach, but she tried desperately to ignore it.

"She's been busy all right," Marnie said, her voice faltering a little. She put her hand on her tummy to calm her nerves and then spit out her big line. "Busy making out with *Matt Heatherly*."

In a flash, Nola's skin turned a stark shade of white that could only be described as "albino chic."

Gotcha.

Sally leaned forward, excited to hear anything that resembled gossip. "Matt Heatherly? *Really?*"

Marnie glanced over at Nola, whose neck was reddening terribly. Lizette had been right. Starting a false rumor about Nola and Matt would teach Nola a lesson she'd never forget about revenge. The stunned look Nola had on her face when Marnie mentioned her Matt crush at Deirdre's party was just the beginning.

Paybacks were a bitch.

"Yes, *really*," Marnie said. "I caught them kissing in the closet at Deirdre's party last Saturday."

Ha! Sally has no idea that was me and *Dane!*

Sally gaped at Nola and stifled a snicker with the palm of her hand. "Wow."

"Uh, that's not true, Marnie, and you know it," a low, unassuming voice muttered.

Marnie turned her head in Evan Sanders's direction. Although his eyes were fixated on his Sidekick as he typed on the keypad at warp speed, the annoyed expression on his face was unmistakable.

Ugh, I have to keep better track of the Whacker crew. Matt and Evan are friends!

"Wait, Evan. Are you calling Marnie a liar?" Sally asked curiously, chomping on the end of her pen.

Marnie's heart rate began to spike. Her false rumor was about to be shot down by Matt's buddy. She had to get Evan out of the picture fast.

However, Marnie couldn't have predicted that Nola would lean over and get right in Marnie's face.

"No, *I* am calling Marnie a liar," Nola snarled.

Marnie's left eyebrow twitched as she pursed her lips tightly. "How dare you call me that after what you did yesterday, you little *skeeze*?!"

Nola backed up, obviously startled by Marnie's harsh words. "You deserved that and more, *chump*!"

When Marnie heard Sally laugh at Nola's diss, she could feel both her eyebrows twitching. This wasn't going as she and Lizette had planned at all. They hadn't expected Nola to be so aggressive and for Evan to come to her aid.

"And you better watch what you say about me — I've got tons of *true* stories about you, the Thong Thief one being the *least* embarrassing!" Nola went on, gnashing her teeth as though she wanted to rip Marnie to shreds.

At that very real and potent threat, Marnie's fight-or-flight response went completely haywire, especially because Sally seemed way too intrigued by what Nola had just said. Marnie was doing all she could to settle down (including a yoga breathing technique that Lizette had taught her) and dish out the cruelest comeback of the twenty-first century, but when push came to shove, the best Marnie could do was raise her hand and ask Mr. Quinn for a hall pass.

As she stormed out of the classroom and into the empty hallway, Marnie couldn't get Nola's victorious grin out of her mind. What was with that girl these days? Was Nola drinking creatine shakes every morning with her shredded wheat and pummeling a punching bag on the weekends? It would explain her newfound ability to stand her ground and turn Marnie into a hall pass–wielding deserter. When Marnie found herself back at her locker, staring mindlessly at her reflection in her small mirror, she was definitely at her wit's end. Her reddening eyes were a clear indicator of that.

Then Marnie saw another reflection besides her own.

"Aw, you missed me, didn't you?"

Weston Briggs was, quite unfortunately, lurking right behind her.

Marnie spun around quickly, expecting that Weston's goofy, conceited smirk would be even wider when they came face-to-face. But what she didn't expect was her favorite guidance counselor, Mrs. Robertson, to be standing next to him.

Instantly, Marnie became flustered. "I have a hall pass," she said, holding it up high.

Smooth, real smooth.

Mrs. Robertson laughed. "Well, that's good, Marnie. I would have hated to write you up."

Marnie smiled halfheartedly.

"Actually, I was just about to bring this new student to your English class," Mrs. Robertson said. "Marnie Fitzpatrick, this is Weston Briggs."

"Oh, we already know each other," Weston said, pulling his Red Sox hat down over his eyes and winking at Marnie mischievously. "In fact, we're good, *good* friends."

God, he is so slimy! Why did I ever let him touch me?

"That's wonderful," Mrs. Robertson replied. "Hey, Marnie, maybe you could be Weston's Best Buddy for the rest of October."

"His *what*?" Marnie could tell from Mrs. Robertson's excited expression that she was about to be forced into joining some ugly school-sanctioned activity.

"In the Best Buddy program, transfer students are paired up with someone else in their class for a couple weeks, so that they can adjust to their new surroundings," Mrs. Robertson said brightly. "Since you two are friends, it seems like a perfect fit."

"I think it's a great idea," Weston said, smiling.

Marnie crumpled up her hall pass in her hand. "Um . . . I don't know. I wouldn't want this to interfere with all of my treasurer-related responsibilities."

"Don't be silly, Marnie. You just have to show Weston around the school and introduce him to people, that kind of thing. Then you both check in with me a few times so we can make sure he feels at home here at Poughkeepsie Central."

Marnie had always thought Mrs. Robertson was a nice lady, despite the fact that she was the reason Marnie had been subjected to Nola Freaking James once a day. But now Marnie believed without a doubt that Mrs.

Robertson was in on some elaborate conspiracy to send her to an early grave. Whether that was true or not, Marnie still felt like she couldn't say no, even though she was screaming it in her head.

"Okay, I guess," Marnie said, dropping her eyes to her steel-toed boots.

"Thanks, Marnie. I really appreciate it," Mrs. Robertson said. "I'm sure this will look great on your transcripts, too."

Yeah, if I don't kill myself by the end of October.

"We should probably head to class," Weston said to Mrs. Robertson.

When Marnie glanced up and saw him trying to stop himself from snickering, she almost kneed him where it counted.

"You're right," Mrs. Robertson said, checking her watch. "I'll expect you two in my office sometime next week with a progress report. Off you go now!"

"This way," Marnie muttered to Weston as she closed her locker door and slunk away from Mrs. Robertson.

Weston had to break into a jog to keep up with Marnie, who was practically sprinting away from him. "Are you mad at me, sweetheart?"

Marnie stopped dead in her tracks and shoved Weston in the shoulder. "*Don't* call me that!"

Weston chuckled loudly. It was obvious that Marnie's temper amused him. "Whatever you say, *Buddy*."

Marnie grunted as she stomped down the hall, her offense shot and her pride wounded not by one but two members of the opposing team.

flowerpower: *hi, nola. whazzup?*
nolaj1994: *nothing much, iris. how r u?*
flowerpower: *ok, just got back from mock trial. i made a witness recant on the stand, it was MAH-VAH-LOUS!*
nolaj1994: *LOL! why am i not surprised?*
flowerpower: *cuz i got the skillz to pay the billz ;-)*
nolaj1994: *u crack me up*
flowerpower: *so r u gonna prepare 4 the soc stud quiz 2morrow?*
nolaj1994: *ugh, yes. all night i'm afraid*
flowerpower: *cool, i'll B right over. need someone to run flash cards with me. u will do*
nolaj1994: *i dunno. it's a madhouse over here*
flowerpower: *so?*
nolaj1994: *so what if u can't concentrate and u get a bad grade on the quiz? it'll B my fault*
flowerpower: *r u mental or something?*
nolaj1994: *hahaha, no, i'm not mental*
flowerpower: *good. a girl like u wouldn't make it one day in the nuthouse*
nolaj1994: *true. i guess i'll c u soon then*
flowerpower: *u will. adios!*

Chapter 13

"I wish Nancy Grace would just shut up already," Iris Santos complained as she munched on some homemade Chex party mix while sitting on Nola's bed. "And she should fire her makeup artist, too. Her mascara is clumpier than Star Jones's!"

Nola smiled and dug her hand into the glass bowl that Iris was holding in between her knees. "I don't think I can watch any more Court TV," she said with her mouth full. "Besides, we're supposed to be studying your flash cards, remember?"

"Meh, one B-plus isn't going to kill our GPAs," Iris said, smirking.

Nola grinned again. When Iris had invited herself over tonight, Nola wasn't sure quite what to expect. She'd mostly spent time with Iris in group situations, and even then, Nola was never 100 percent comfortable around her because she was just so . . . in your face. Iris always called a spade a spade, too. On some occasions, Nola thought that was an admirable trait, but at other times, it was really off-putting. However, for the past couple of hours, she had gotten along pretty well with Iris. Then again, they'd been immersed in a best of

Nancy Grace marathon and were only speaking to each other during commercial breaks. There was still a chance that things could go sour.

"You're right. Two hours of Nancy is more than enough." Iris leaned forward and grabbed the remote, which was lying next to Nola's white-socked feet. She hit the OFF button and turned toward Nola. "What do you want to do now?"

A worried expression formed on Nola's face. Even though she had verbally hound-slapped Marnie earlier today, Nola couldn't shake this ominous and paranoid feeling. Not only was she concerned that Sally might spread that stupid false rumor Marnie tried to start, but she was also scared that anyone could be capable of betraying her like Marnie had. It was bad enough that every time Nola saw Marnie in school, it was like reliving each moment in which Marnie had disappointed her. Now that Iris was here hanging out in her room like Marnie used to, Nola was suddenly fearful that she might be putting herself at risk all over again.

On the other hand, maybe it was wrong for Nola to assume that becoming better friends with Iris would open her up to a world of hurt. In fact, Iris and Marnie couldn't be more different — the biggest difference being that Iris wasn't a popularity-chasing wannabe.

She was just herself, no matter what anyone had to say about it. Which was why Nola decided she should act the exact same way.

"Want to play *Scene It?*" she asked Iris enthusiastically, hopping off the bed and skipping to her entertainment center, where all her DVDs were kept.

"Wait a second. Does this game involve yelling at the TV?" Iris asked as she tossed a piece of Wheat Chex into the air and caught it in her mouth.

Nola grabbed the box and grinned. "Sure does."

"Then you are in for an ass-kicking, girlfriend!" Iris yelped.

"I think not, Miss Santos," Nola chuckled as she opened the box and took out the first disk. "I am the undefeated *Scene It* champion."

Iris rolled her eyes. "Your last opponent wears *thongs*. No wonder you won all the time."

Oh, my God, Iris just ranked on Marnie! This girl is beyond cool!

"You just better lay off that 'Miss Santos' crap. If Matt ever hears you stealing his lines, he'll know how much you worship him," Iris quipped as she braided the mane of Billy the Lion, Nola's favorite stuffed animal.

Nola tried to hide the fact that Iris's smart-mouthed comment had stung her like an angry wasp, but Iris looked up just in time to see Nola in full-blown mop-ing mode.

"Oh, c'mon, Nola. I was just messing with you." Iris pulled off her argyle socks, balled them up, and threw them on Nola's floor as though she was in her own room.

Nola wanted to explain to Iris that her feelings about Matt were a forbidden subject and something that she could only talk about with her best friend. But as she stood there holding a *Scene It* DVD, Nola reminded herself that right now Marnie Fitzpatrick was her worst enemy, and her temporary best friend was off some-where with his father in the middle of a great mystery. Actually, if there was one person who seemed to know Matt really well, it was Iris. Perhaps Nola could dig for some dirt (in a harmless, noninvasive, non-*Riley* way) and find out where he was and what he was doing. At least, it would get them off the topic of Nola worship-ping him, right?

The sound of Nola's bedroom door creaking open made her snap to attention.

"Hey, sorry to bother you guys."

Argh! Can't this dweeb ever leave me alone?!

Iris shot up off of Nola's bed and trotted over to the door. Then she hiked up her gray corduroy skirt a little so it rose up above her slightly scabby knees.

Okay, maybe she and Marnie aren't as different as I thought.

"You're not bothering us at all," Iris replied sweetly as she shook her long shiny bangs out of her almond-shaped eyes. "What's up?"

Ian opened the door farther, but with a bit of hesitation. Apparently, he could sense that Nola didn't feel the same way Iris did about the interruption. "I'm making Boca burgers for the boys. Do you want any?"

Nola pushed up the sleeves of her chunky blue cardigan and sneered at Ian, who was dressed in his traditional sweater-vest–button-down shirt with jeans combo. If he thought he could use food as a way to lure her into the kitchen and keep tabs on her, he was sorely mistaken!

"No, thanks. We're not hungry," she said sharply.

Just then Iris turned around and gave Nola a look that could only be read as *YOU ARE A GIGANTIC IDIOT!*

Iris spun back toward Ian and flashed him a smile. "I'd love a burger, actually."

Ian scratched at his ear and glanced at Nola apprehensively. "You sure you don't want one?"

"I said no, didn't I?" Nola said.

Iris immediately jumped in to do damage control. "Don't mind Nola. She just ate a lot of Chex party mix. I think it made her gassy."

Nola's mouth went agape as she felt two hives swell up on her forearm.

Did she just say I was GASSY?

"Um, okay," Ian said with a slight smirk. "I'll let you know when your burger is done."

"Just holla!" Iris chirped as she closed the door behind him. A second later, she was on Nola like white on rice. "What's the matter with you? You made me look *fat* in front of your brother!"

Nola's hands flew to her hips. "First of all, Ian is SO not my brother! He's my twin brothers' *babysitter!*"

"Who cares? He's *hotter* than any of the guys in *High School Musical!*" Iris spat. "And I sounded like a hog asking for a burger after you said 'We're not hungry'!"

Nola's lower lip was trembling as she tried to hold back her laughter. "You think *Ian* is *hot?*"

"Nola, let's do the math. Gorgeous eyes plus amazing smile plus Johnny Depp cheekbones equals *too damn hot!*" Iris threw up her arms in frustration. "Obviously, you're in need of some serious tutoring."

All of a sudden, Nola wasn't able to prevent herself from bursting into laughter, and soon Iris was stumbling toward Nola in a fit of hysterics that had them propping each other up.

"I'm sorry, I just don't see it, Iris," Nola chuckled as she held her aching side.

"You're too blinded by dumb Matt love." Iris yanked on Nola's ponytail. "It's why you can't even see that Ian is lusting after *your* kibbles and bits."

Nola stopped laughing instantly. "Lusting after my *what*?"

"Wow, I thought I was exaggerating when I used the word *dumb*," Iris said, wandering over to Nola's mirror and checking out her teeth. "I bet that isn't the first time Ian's used an excuse to come up to your room and talk to you."

Nola was having a hard time breathing for some reason, so she took a few steps backward and flopped down on her desk chair. Then she realized that the *Scene It* DVD was still in her hand.

Suddenly, Nola wasn't obsessing about her Marnie grudge, Riley's peculiar e-mail, or Matt's mystifying past. The only thing she could think about now was how something could be right in front of her face without her ever really noticing it.

Chapter 14

MUST-HAVES FOR MY DATE WITH DANE
1) Oral-B Brush-Ups — to prevent smelly breath or get rid of anything that might become stuck between my teeth at dinner
2) Travel-size Powder Fresh scent Dove deodorant — don't want smelly/sweaty pits, either! Gross!
3) The kewl chocolate brown cami-cardigan twinset from FCUK. Paired with whitewash DKNY peep-toe flats
4) My favorite delicate multistranded beaded necklace — just try to forget that Nola made it!

As Marnie sat in the passenger seat of Dane Harris's cobalt blue Jaguar convertible, which was traveling quickly on Poughkeepsie's back roads, she thought about how far she'd come since the first day of high school and smiled. A few short weeks ago, Marnie had reserved Friday nights for sleepovers at Nola's house, where she and her ex-best friend would watch movies and eat Chex party mix and give each other pedicures and giggle at silly jokes.

All of it seemed so childish and immature to Marnie now. Dane had just taken her out to a very expensive dinner at Beach Tree Grill, a beautiful restaurant near Vassar. He'd insisted that Marnie get whatever she wanted — she couldn't resist the sautéed tiger shrimp or the vanilla crème brûlée — and when the check came, he put down his very own platinum credit card. While Marnie was used to money being thrown around — Lizette was always tearing through her father's royalty checks — it wasn't the same as when a boy like Dane lavished a lot of attention and cash on her. She felt so sophisticated and worldly and grown-up. Like she belonged at those fancy soirees at the country club that Dane attended with his family. Like she was just as good as Lizette.

Dane shifted into another gear, causing the car to accelerate and the wind to whip Marnie's blonde hair into her face. As the music from the radio bellowed from the speakers, she flipped down the visor and looked at herself in the illuminated mirror. Marnie frowned when she saw that half of her cute little updo had fallen out. Not only that, but her mascara was running because her eyes were tearing so much from the strong air current.

Marnie flipped the visor back up and sighed. Lizette Levin would never, *ever* show her face looking like this. Or have eaten a full plate of food in front of a gorgeous guy. Even so, Marnie tried to push any thoughts of Lizette out of her mind tonight. She was with *her* gorgeous guy, and planned on enjoying it, regardless of Lizette's recent chumminess with Dane or anything else that might ruin the moment (for instance, thinking about the twenty or so times she had to tell that no-good Best Buddy of hers, Weston, "Get lost or die!" within a seven-hour span.)

"We're almost there," Dane said, glancing over to Marnie and smirking.

Marnie grinned in return. Dane looked so amazing tonight. He was wearing a dark gray Theory blazer over a light blue shirt and black pants that broke perfectly at the ankles. He'd put a bit of Bed Head pomade in his hair — Marnie could tell from the scent — so it was even stiffer and spikier, like Sawyer's.

Dah! Don't think about him, *either!*

Marnie shook her head and tried focusing on the scenery. "Where is *there* exactly?"

"Can't you tell yet?" Dane gripped the steering wheel and gunned the gas when they came to a straightaway.

Since there weren't many streetlights on these country roads and Dane was driving like he was outrunning the law, Marnie had difficulty making out anything but lots and lots of trees. However, when the Jag began to slow down and turned around a bend, she realized that Dane had brought her back to Morgan Lake.

Marnie put her hand on Dane's knee and squeezed. "What are you up to?"

He made a strange face, like he was confused or distracted, and downshifted so the car jerked a little. "You'll see."

"Are you sure it's safe for you to be driving this?" Marnie said, giggling.

"Well, my dad thinks so. He gave it to me as a gift when I got my learner's permit."

Marnie tried to quell a pinch of anxiety. "You only have a *permit?*"

"Hey, I've been pulled over before. The cops always let me go."

If that line had come out of any other guy's mouth, Marnie would have thought he was obnoxious. Instead, Dane sounded confident and powerful. Marnie never quite noticed how much being close to him made her feel like that, too.

All of a sudden, the Jag turned into a tiny lot in front of a familiar dock, which jutted out into the lake. It was the spot where Dane and Marnie had shared their first kiss. The dock was lined with white Christmas lights so it glowed magnificently in the dark.

"Oh, Dane, this is incredible." Marnie felt as though her heart was going to jump right out of her chest.

Dane put the Jag in park, then leaned over to Marnie and brushed his lips gently near her left ear. "We're just getting started."

"We are?" she whispered.

Dane smiled and ran his finger lightly down her nose. Leaning back in his seat, he turned off the engine but kept the headlights on. Next, he pulled out an iPod from the dashboard and hooked it up to the Jag's stereo. While he scrolled through a list of songs, Marnie fidgeted in her leather seat with excitement. After a minute, Dane finally hit the PLAY button and "Each Other" by Katharine McPhee echoed out into the unseasonably warm October air.

Oh. My. GOD! This is . . .

"Your favorite song, right?" Dane asked.

"Yeah, it is. How did you know?"

"Lizette told me," he said simply, tugging on a strand of her hair.

Marnie tried to stop her lower lip from trembling by biting it gently. "Lizette, huh?"

"Well, now that we're here, I guess it's safe to tell you." Dane rubbed Marnie's knee affectionately. "Lizette has been helping me plan this evening all week."

"Really?" Marnie was both extremely relieved and excited when she heard this news.

"I wanted tonight to be perfect, so who better to ask for tips than your best friend?" Dane leaned in and kissed her cheek, then her mouth, then her neck.

Even though Marnie knew she should be bouncing off the walls right now, she felt very guilty. All this time, Lizette had been helping Dane make Marnie's romantic dream date come true, and here Marnie had been suspecting them of the worst. How could she have even thought for a minute that either one of them would con her like that? As Dane worked his lips back to her mouth, she couldn't remember exactly why.

Dane pulled away a little, but his hand kept rubbing her knee. "So do you want to dance?"

Marnie's eyes widened with surprise. "Here? *Now?*"

"Yeah, you got a problem with that?" Dane said playfully.

"Of course not," Marnie laughed.

Dane got out of the Jag and took his jacket off, throwing it in the backseat. Then he rolled up his sleeves, ever so sexily. Marnie was feeling very warm herself and she contemplated leaving her sweater behind. But when she exited the car and looked down at her chest, she changed her mind. Her thin cami was a bit too revealing all by itself.

Dane opened his arms up wide as if he was expecting a hug. "I'm waiting."

Marnie grinned so hard she could feel the strain on her cheeks. She strolled over to Dane slowly while tossing him a flirty look. When she was inches away from him, she took Dane's hands and placed them on her hips. Then Marnie reached up and placed her hands on his shoulders.

Dane began swaying to the music, gripping Marnie tightly but not too tight. She was delighted that he had a little bit of rhythm and wasn't afraid to show it. When Marnie put her head against his chest, she could hear his heart beating rapidly, just as hers was. Apparently, no matter how calm and cool either of them appeared on the outside, on the inside, they were nervous . . . and happy. At least, that was how Marnie felt, anyway.

"Am I passing your slow-dancing litmus test or what?" she heard Dane ask.

"With flying colors," Marnie replied. "In fact, you're even better than you were at Tucker's luau."

"Does that mean you'll go to Homecoming with me?"

Marnie stopped moving and pulled back a bit so she could look Dane in the eyes and make sure he wasn't kidding. "Um . . . what?"

"Okay, one more time." Dane's smile was completely effortless. "Will you, Marnie Fitzpatrick, the loveliest girl in school, go to the Homecoming dance with me?"

Marnie wanted to say Yes so badly she could scream, but Yes didn't seem to convey how thrilled she was that he'd asked her. No one else, including Weston Briggs, had ever made her feel this . . . *coveted* before. So Marnie did what any girl would do in her shoes — she got up on her tiptoes and kissed him.

As the song died out a few minutes later and their kissing became more intense, Marnie vowed never to doubt Dane or her best friend again.

Chapter 15

It was a dreary and rainy Saturday afternoon, the perfect weather for jewelry making on the window seat, or so Nola had thought. It was also one of the rare days that her mom and dad were both off work at the same time, which was why they took Dennis and Dylan to the circus for some family bonding. Even though they practically begged her to come, Nola opted out of the Ringling Brothers adventure. Not because she was an animal activist like Iris. She just wanted some peace so she could channel all of her energy into a new project.

However, for the past hour Nola had been sprawled out on the window seat, swimming in a sea of beads, chains, wires, and gemstones, and she hadn't made one single thing. Instead, she wound up watching hundreds of raindrops streak the glass pane in front of her, thinking about the last big storm to hit Poughkeepsie.

Nola couldn't help but laugh to herself as she remembered how Dennis and Dylan had locked her and Matt out of the house as it started to pour. The memory was so vivid, it was as if she and Matt had gotten caught in the rain just a few minutes ago. But the reality was that Nola hadn't seen or heard from Matt for three whole days. As she wrote his name on the foggy window,

Nola tried not to worry about him too much. He'd vanished before and returned in one piece. This disappearance wasn't any different. Soon, Matt would be back at school and everything would be normal again.

Nola wiped away Matt's name with a brisk stroke of her palm. She was a fool if she thought she could convince herself that being status quo with Matt Heatherly was enough for her. Although it seemed like he and Riley might have hit a rough patch (and that assumption was a stretch of the imagination), they were still *boyfriend and girlfriend*. Whatever he may have said to Nola on the phone on Wednesday under the guise of pseudo-best friendship, none of it really mattered when she couldn't really get close to him. And without Marnie or anyone else to confide in, Nola had no choice but to keep her feelings bottled up inside.

Thankfully, only one or two tears crawled down Nola's flushed cheeks before she heard the sound of the key in the front door. She glanced at her watch and tapped on the face of it, thinking it must be running fast. There was no way the circus could be over already, unless of course Dylan and Dennis wreaked havoc under the big tent, which wouldn't surprise her in the least.

"Hi, Nola."

Ian Capshaw was standing in the entryway to the living room, his belted Burberry trench coat dripping beads of water onto the floor and his navy blue umbrella still wide open.

Although Nola was warm in her favorite red North Face fleece pullover and a pair of charcoal gray yoga pants, she shivered when she saw him. Ever since Iris made that crack about Ian wanting her "kibbles and bits" on Thursday, Nola had been making herself scarce whenever Ian was in proximity. Not that she believed Iris's nonsense. Later that night, Iris had psyched Nola out with at least ten bogus stories and then shouted "Gotcha!" as soon as Nola was reeled in good. It was ridiculous to even suggest that Ian had a thing for her, anyway. He couldn't stand Nola, and she couldn't stand him. That was that.

After staring at Nola a little too long, Ian looked down and noticed that he hadn't closed his umbrella. Then he groaned. "So how many years of bad luck is this? Ten or twenty?"

Well, isn't he as charming as ever?

"You're thinking of a broken mirror. That's seven years of bad luck," Nola replied as she tried to appear busy and uninterested in anything Ian had to say.

"Huh. But an open umbrella in a house is just general bad luck for an unlimited length of time?"

Nola rolled her eyes as she picked up a purple stone out of a pile. "Beats me."

Ian closed the umbrella, then shrugged off his coat, revealing a loose-fitting Abercrombie T-shirt and pale blue jeans. He hung his items on the hooks in the hallway and came back into the living room, rubbing his hands in anticipation.

"So, where are the hellions? Waiting to clobber me, right?" Ian's eyes darted around as though he was seconds away from a Terrible Twins guerrilla attack.

"No, they're at the circus with my parents," Nola said, exchanging the stone in her hand for some colorful beads.

"Oh, crap," Ian groaned. "I think I got my Saturdays mixed up."

"Looks that way," Nola mumbled.

Ian crossed the room and leaned against the wall near the window, peering down at her with scrutiny. "Are you in the middle of something?"

"What do you think?"

"I don't know. That's why I *asked*."

"Well, it's *kind of obvious,* isn't it?"

"Not really!"

Nola threw her hands up in the air, utterly frustrated and annoyed. "God, Ian! The boys aren't here, so why don't you just *leave*?!"

A vein in Ian's forehead started to bulge, but

somehow he managed to still look really cute. "That's a *great* idea!"

As soon as he turned on his heels, a wave of remorse pulled Nola off the shore of self-pity and almost drowned her. All Ian had done was show up on the wrong day and she had acted like a whiny brat. True, there was something about Ian that brought out the worst in Nola, but this time he didn't deserve to be chewed out.

"Wait, Ian!" Nola yelled.

Ian paused for a moment but didn't turn around. Nola sprang up from the window seat and hurried over to him. The scowl on Ian's face was so severe she didn't think he'd stick around to hear her apologize. But for some strange reason, she was panicky at the thought of him walking out the door, hopping in his BMW, and driving back to his dorm at Vassar.

"I'm *really* sorry I laid into you like that," Nola said nervously. "I'm just . . . just . . ."

Ian raised an eyebrow and smirked. "A mean girl?"

"I'm *not* mean!" Nola squawked. "I'm . . . nice."

"No, you aren't."

"Yes, I am!"

"No, you're *not*. And I can prove it, too."

Nola's shoulders slumped forward, indicating intense fatigue. "I'm dying to know how, Ian."

"Well, let's spend the rest of the day together. My guess is you won't last an hour without being mean to me," he said smugly.

Nola didn't even crack a smile. "Are you kidding? I could be nice to you *forever*! That doesn't mean you won't get on every single one of my nerves."

"Make that a half hour," Ian said with a superior grin.

He is such a pompous ass! I'll show him just how nice *I am!*

Nola narrowed her eyes at Ian and held out her hand confidently. "You're on."

After driving for ten minutes in Ian's BMW, Nola was pretty sure she was going to lose the bet she'd just made. Not only was Ian the slowest, most cautious driver she'd ever seen, but he also had the worst taste in music. What too-cute-for-his-own-good, know-it-all seventeen-year-old boy would crank up the soft jazz station on their car stereo? Apparently, Ian Capshaw. Nola was trying hard not to reach over and start channel surfing until she found something decent to listen to, but she knew that would probably spark another fight, so instead she sat on her hands and gazed out the window.

"Aren't you curious about where we're going?" Nola heard Ian ask.

"Not really," she muttered.

"What did you say?"

Nola turned toward Ian and gave him a wide albeit forced smile. "I said, 'Wherever we go, I'm sure we'll have a barrel of laughs.'"

"Right," Ian said, rolling his eyes.

"What? I was being nice."

Ian made a left at a busy intersection. "Oh, is that what you were being?"

Nola took a deep breath and clenched her teeth. She could tell that Ian was trying to bait her into an argument and she had to stay strong. Her pride depended on it.

"I'll try to seem more sincere," she replied.

"Much appreciated, Nola," Ian said, chuckling. "All right, here we are."

Nola looked out the window as Ian pulled into a large parking lot filled with cars. She gazed upward at the beautiful stone building with stained-glass windows that loomed before them. Ian parked the car, and the engine stopped purring.

"Okay, let's go," he said.

"Wait a second, Ian. Why are we at *church*?" Nola knew this had to be some kind of trick.

"Because we're getting married," he said with a straight face.

Instantly, Iris's "kibbles and bits" comment from

the other day started ringing in Nola's ears. She thought about escaping the clutches of her obviously insane family babysitter, but when Ian began laughing uncontrollably, all she wanted to do was clock him in the jaw.

"Seriously, just come inside and you'll see why we're here." Ian opened the car door and got out, but when he noticed that Nola wasn't budging, he leaned down and peered inside the car. "You know, nice people usually have a sense of humor."

"I have a *freaking great* sense of humor," Nola grumbled quietly as she got out of the BMW.

Ian tossed his keys up into the air repeatedly as he walked to the church. Nola trailed behind him by a few paces, anxiously toying with the zipper of her Columbia windbreaker. She had no idea what Ian had in store for her. Worst-case scenario was that he was taking Nola to see a priest for an old-fashioned exorcism.

However, that seemed out of the question when Ian changed course. Instead of going up the stairs to the church, he darted left toward the community center, where a few people were exiting with shopping bags. Nola grinned a little bit when Ian held the door open for her after doing so for a gray-haired middle-aged man who was carrying a wrought-iron floor lamp. Yet the grin expanded into an authentic smile once Nola wandered into the auditorium-size room and realized that

Ian had brought her to a very quirky senior citizens' flea market.

There were scores of people bustling about and strolling through the rows of tables that held tons of merchandise, antiques, and . . . junk. Nola looked to her right and spied a woman selling wooden crucifixes, then glanced to her left and watched a man exchange his money for an album full of baseball cards.

It wasn't Prince Street in Soho, but it was still pretty cool.

"So, what do you think?" Ian asked, his voice tinged with apprehension.

"It's great," Nola said, brimming with enthusiasm. "I can't wait to wander around."

Ian elongated his neck and scanned the white-haired crowd. "Go ahead. I have to help someone at their booth, anyway."

Nola tossed Ian a confused look. He had to help someone at the flea market? "Well, could you use an extra person?"

See, I am nice.

"Um, sure." Ian seemed a little unsettled, like he wasn't too thrilled to accept Nola's offer. Still, he waved her along as he made his way down one of the aisles.

Nola couldn't resist poking around at a few of the tables as she followed in Ian's footsteps. There were so many tchotchkes and knickknacks and odds and ends, it looked as though her grandparents' attic had just thrown up everywhere. Actually, this flea market kind of reminded Nola of the garage sales she and junior-high-era Marnie used to go to on Sunday afternoons, where they'd hunt for bargain clothes or antique gems. Needless to say, Nola found herself being drawn in by the kitschy vibe in the air, reminding her of days spent with someone who understood her without even trying.

When Nola caught up to Ian, he was talking to an elderly African-American woman in a wheelchair who was working two tables. The woman had on a heavy knit sweater, and a light blue blanket was wrapped around her legs. Nola also noticed that while the lady's skin was wrinkled and her glasses were gigantic, she appeared quite young because of the way she was clowning around with Ian.

"I'm telling you, I think Moses might have duped us with the Ten Commandments," the old woman said.

Ian grabbed a box from underneath the table and opened it with a razor blade. "That sounds like blasphemy to me," he remarked.

Nola closed in on the table and cleared her throat so she could make her presence known. "Need a hand with that?" she asked Ian.

The woman squinted at her. "You should give him two hands, honey. The boy is incredibly clumsy."

"I am not," Ian said, his cheeks flushing with embarrassment.

"So who's this pretty thing? Your girlfriend?" The old woman smacked her lips and smiled.

Now Ian's cheeks were a shade of fire engine red. "Don't be silly. She's a kid. I just babysit her and her little brothers."

"Well, how unfortunate for you, Ian." The woman extended her hand to Nola. "I'm Esther, child. Who might you be?"

Nola leaned over the table and shook Esther's hand, which was soft like flower petals. "I'm Nola."

"Is this your first time to the flea market?"

"Yes, it is." The sound of Esther's voice was so sweet and calming that Nola almost forgot to be nervous when chatting with strangers.

"Well, Ian will give you the professional tour, since he's here almost every Saturday," Esther said as Ian unloaded a few items wrapped in tissue paper. "He helps a lot of the folks with their tables."

He is here *every Saturday? To help* old people?

Nola figured that Ian was more of an "I'm studying in the library all weekend" type of guy, not an "I'm

volunteering my brawn to the elderly at a flea market"
type of guy.

"You're my favorite, Esther. Don't forget that," Ian
said with a wink.

"Not everyone is going to debate religion with me
like you do, that's for sure," Esther said to Ian before
pointing at Nola. "Can you believe Ian comes to the
church hall every Saturday when he should be at the syn-
agogue? He's a heathen, but I still adore him."

Nola was amazed at how contagious Esther's energy
was. Right now, she was feeling like she could adore
Ian, too. Of course, only someday far, far in the future,
like when they were Esther's age. Or older.

"Would you mind unwrapping this?" Ian handed
Nola a tissue-paper-covered object.

Nola nodded and undid the tissue paper carefully.
Inside were a set of salt and pepper shakers in the shape
of two pigs. She placed them on the table and giggled
when she realized that everything on Esther's table
were salt and pepper shakers in a variety of shapes,
colors, and sizes. There were shakers that looked like
the Eiffel Tower and ones that resembled both fat and
thin Elvises. It was too cute for words.

Nola looked up at Ian as he continued to unpack
boxes. He seemed very preoccupied with the task at
hand, but a couple of times his eyes shifted in her

direction and he smiled a little. It was almost as if he was happy to be in her company, and oddly enough, Nola was feeling like that might be true for her, too.

"Why don't you two kids run along?" Esther said after Nola unwrapped a few more shakers. "I'm sure Nola wants to check out the jewelry."

Nola's breath caught in her throat. "How did you know —"

"Yeah, let me take you around, Nola. We can help Esther later," Ian said hurriedly.

Esther let out a hearty laugh as Ian dragged Nola away by the arm. Once they were about ten feet from Esther's table, Ian let go of Nola and loosened up a little.

"Sorry about Esther. She's a little off her rocker sometimes," he said.

"No, I think she's great," Nola replied as she strolled over to a vendor who was selling handmade stained-glass mobiles. She gazed at one that was made of dangling butterflies and grinned. "This *place* is great, actually. Being here certainly makes it easier to be nice to you."

Ian chuckled. "That was my intention."

Nola looked over her shoulder at Ian. "Really?"

"Well, that and I had to help Esther out with a few things." Ian walked over toward Nola and gently touched a star-themed mobile with his index finger. "Wow, I've never seen anything so colorful."

"I know. Imagine what it's like when the light shines through it," Nola said.

"The jewelry tables are in the back. Want to check those out?"

"Yeah, that would be great."

Ian led her over to a couple of tables where two young, artsy women were sitting on metal folding chairs and gabbing about some friend of theirs who had dropped off the face of the earth after meeting a guy. Once Nola saw the jewelry they were selling, she immediately stopped eavesdropping on their conversation. They had a bunch of vintage pieces, including a few broaches and strands of black pearls, as well as some costume and handmade jewelry. Nola was mesmerized by all of it.

Ian nudged her with his elbow. "See anything you like?"

It was strange and utterly disturbing. When Nola heard him ask that, she thought to herself, *Yeah, you.* But how could that be? Less than an hour ago, she and Ian were at each other's throats. Was it at all possible that she could be friends with someone who drove her crazy? And if the answer was yes, then did that mean Nola and Marnie could ever get past all the pain of the past few weeks and make up? Although Nola was still furious with her ex-best friend, she couldn't seem to ignore the little voice in her head that would remind her of how good she and Marnie had had it for years.

"I like . . . everything," she replied softly.

"Well, I'm hungry. You want to get something to eat?"

"Sure."

On their way to the snack bar, Nola felt her cell phone vibrating in her bag.

"Hold on, Ian. I'm getting a call."

He reached into his back pocket for his black leather wallet. "Why don't I go get us some pierogi and applesauce?"

"Okay, thanks."

While Ian strode off, Nola dug out her cell phone, which was tangled up in her iPod earbud wires. Once she managed to separate the two, she flipped open her phone without even looking at the caller ID.

"Hello?"

"Hey, it's me."

Oh, my God. Matt.

Nola moved out of the bustle of the crowd to a quieter area so she could hear better. "Hey. How are you?"

"Uh, not good." Matt's voice sounded very strained, like he had a sore throat.

Nola put a finger in her left ear to block out the bickering of two women who were stationed at the quilting table. "What's wrong?"

"Where are you?"

Nola glanced around to see if Ian was in earshot. "Oh, I'm at a flea market. Looking at . . . stuff."

"Well, can you talk?" Matt's tone had gone from gravelly to sad in a matter of seconds.

"Yeah, go ahead," Nola urged. She knew it was awful to imagine her and Matt living out Marnie's closet makeout lie at a time like this, but she couldn't help it.

Matt inhaled deeply as though he was about to launch into a monologue. But before he could say anything, Ian tapped on Nola's shoulder.

"I forgot to ask if you wanted your pierogi fried or boiled?" Ian asked.

"Wait, hold on a second," Nola said to Matt. She put her hand over the mouthpiece and stared at Ian. "Which is better?"

"Fried, definitely," Ian responded.

"All right, fried then," Nola said, trying to hurry Ian along. Once he walked away, she returned to her phone call. "Sorry about that. I'm ready now."

"No problem." Matt coughed a few times and sighed. "You see, my dad and I —"

Nola felt another tap on her shoulder. It had to be

Ian. Sure enough when she turned around it was him. "Hold on again, Matt."

"Ugh, fine," she heard Matt say in frustration.

Nola covered the mouthpiece and leered at Ian. "What now?"

"Just wanted to know if you were thirsty." From the smirk on his face, Ian seemed confident that Nola was going to lash out at him with only a few minutes left to go in their bet.

But Nola wasn't going to give in to Ian, especially because she'd made it this far without cracking. "A Coke would be *nice*. Thank you very much, Ian."

He smiled. "One Coke, coming right up."

As soon as Ian left, Nola quickly got back to Matt. "Sorry about the interruption, Matt. What were you saying?"

There was an awkward silence that made Nola very nervous.

"Why don't we just talk later? You sound busy," Matt said kind of gruffly.

"No, I'm not!" Nola realized she sounded too eager, but she couldn't control her tone. The last thing she wanted to do was turn Matt off now — she'd been waiting to hear from him for so long, and it seemed as though he was about to confide in her.

"It's okay. I'll call you back," Matt said softly.

One of the things Nola had learned about Matt since making him her backup best friend was that he had trouble staying true to his word. It was the quality she liked least. Nevertheless, it wasn't coming between Nola and her feelings for Matt and, as she stood there quietly on the phone, she wondered if anything ever *would* come between them.

"Who wants some hot pierogi?"

Nola's eyes darted to her left. Ian sidled up next to her with a paper plate filled with pierogi and applesauce in one hand and a large Coke in the other. Even though she wanted to keep talking with Matt, she wasn't about to tell Ian to get lost. Actually, once the tasty aroma hit Nola's nostrils, she kind of wanted to share the food with Ian rather than drag information out of Matt, only to find herself disappointed as usual.

"I'll talk to you later, Matt," Nola said into the phone.

And then Matt was gone.

Chapter 16

Marnie's Sunday morning run was of epic proportions. Not only had she tacked on five more miles than usual, but she'd also cut her time down an average of twenty seconds per mile. As her legs propelled her forward at what seemed like a cheetah's pace, Marnie checked out her sports watch and put two fingers on a vein in her neck. Her pulse was accelerating a little each time her New Balance sneakers pressed down on the pavement beneath her. But when Marnie reached the finish line, which was the entrance to Wayras Park, she was glad that she'd outlasted one of her greatest competitors — her mother.

Marnie smiled as she stretched her hamstrings and watched her mom stagger toward her, drenched in sweat and gasping for air. Mrs. Fitzpatrick had been a formidable athlete in college and had medaled in several triathlons. Every so often Mrs. Fitzpatrick would ask to tag along on Marnie's runs, just to see if she still "had it." After gaining some confidence, her mom would usually challenge Marnie to a race, which Marnie had always lost, but by a very close margin.

Today was different, though. Marnie had such a spring in her step, it was as if she had two urban-rebounding trampolines attached to her feet. She felt so invigorated and alive that she didn't even mind that she'd tripped and scraped her knee a mile back, tearing a small hole in her favorite blue Fila track pants.

Her mom finally made it to the park entrance and collapsed on a nearby bench, completely out of breath. She wiped the perspiration off her brow and said, "Didn't I teach you not to gloat?"

Marnie laughed. "I'm not gloating, Mom."

"Then why the big grin?"

Marnie snickered again as she put her hands on the top of the bench, leaned forward, and stretched out her calves. There were two reasons for the big grin. First of all, her date with Dane on Friday had been *spectacular*. She'd never been romanced like that before — the expensive dinner, the moonlit (and illegal!) drive up to Morgan Lake, and their beautiful slow dance in front of the headlights of Dane's Jaguar convertible. Thinking about all of that now was giving Marnie severe hot flashes, which were going unnoticed by her hyperventilating mom.

And then there was reason number two: Lizette Levin wasn't messing around with Dane. In fact, Marnie called Lizette as soon as he had dropped her off and thanked her profusely for helping him plan the evening. It felt so good to have that weight of suspicion lifted off her shoulders, especially when the three unrelated members of the Axis of Evil (i.e., Nola, Brynne, and Weston) were doing everything in their power to crush her. Now Marnie could focus on what really counted, like scheduling dress-shopping sprees with Lizette in New York City and protecting her position in Poughkeepsie Central's social stratosphere.

"Well, I'm grinning because I finally got asked to Homecoming," Marnie said, her voice high and squeaky with excitement.

Suddenly, her mom was as chipper as a robin. "Really? That's wonderful!"

Marnie and her mom shared a sticky hug. "I know! I can't wait."

"I'm positive you'll be on the freshman class Homecoming court, just like Erin was," her mother beamed as she retied her shoelace.

Marnie sighed. Would there *ever* be a time when she didn't get compared to her sister?

"And she'll be home that weekend to hand over her crown and be in the parade," Mrs. Fitzpatrick said, standing up and looking in toward the park. "Won't that be so much fun?"

"Yeah. What a thrill," Marnie said flatly.

For a moment, Marnie wished that her father had run with her instead. But she hadn't seen or heard from him in at least a week. Settling into his new postdivorce apartment in Connecticut had taken a lot longer than he intended, or so his last e-mail said. Marnie swallowed hard when she thought ahead to the dance and Dane coming over to her house to get their picture taken. She wondered if her father would even be there, snapping away with his digital camera. More often than not, her dad seemed to have other, more pressing obligations to tend to, so it was doubtful at best.

However, if her father did show up to chronicle the occasion, Marnie realized that he would ask about Nola and why she wasn't hiding in the corner of their living room, wearing some fancy frock that Marnie would have had to force her into. Marnie hadn't told him that she and Nola weren't on good terms anymore, or that they were pretty much fighting with each other on a regular basis. She figured the less her dad knew the better. Besides, Mrs. Fitzpatrick seemed kind of pleased that her daughter was branching out and forming new friend-ships, especially with a popular girl like Lizette.

"So which boy asked you?" Marnie heard her mom say.

She tightened her ponytail holder and readjusted the straps on her hot-pink tank top (with a built in sup-port bra, of course). "What do you mean, which boy?"

Since Friday night, one guy had a Microsoft-like

monopoly over her thoughts, and his name was Dane Harris.

"Oh, I thought that boy over there was a contender," her mom said, pointing to the skate park in the distance.

Marnie rolled her neck and straightened her posture as she walked over to her mom. She was loosened up and relaxed until she followed the direction of her mother's finger and saw Sawyer Lee performing daredevil stunts all alone on the half-pipes.

"No," Marnie mumbled, remembering how Sawyer's hand felt in hers only a few days ago. "He wasn't."

Her mom let out a long, deep breath. "Okay, let's head back to the house. You can fill me in over breakfast."

Marnie watched Sawyer pivot quickly on his skateboard. *Maybe I should go say hi . . . just for a sec.*

"You go ahead, I'll catch up," she said.

"I'm sure you will, Speedy Gonzales," her mom replied, swatting Marnie on the butt teasingly.

As soon as Mrs. Fitzpatrick was down the block, Marnie began pulling herself together. She took the bottom of her tank and blotted her shiny cheeks, forehead, and chin. Then she licked her lips so they weren't so dry and chapped-looking. Marnie brought her shoulders back and extended her spine up toward the sky, so that she'd appear confident and at least an inch taller.

Her New Balance sneakers trod lightly on the path leading to the skate park, and the early morning breeze was cool enough to make Marnie cross her arms over her chest and stroke her arms with her hands. Usually she'd get too warm in a sweatshirt during her runs, but now she wished that she'd brought one along. Even so, as she closed in on Sawyer, another round of hot flashes rushed through Marnie.

And she wasn't thinking about Dane and their fabulous date at all.

When Marnie hit the cement of the skate park, Sawyer's ink-colored eyes caught her own. He smiled immediately and she reciprocated, until Sawyer skidded on his back wheels and stopped so close to Marnie that she jumped back and yelped.

"How'd you know I'd be here?" Sawyer said, pulling the backward baseball cap he was wearing down to his small, almost delicate ears.

Marnie looked at his stomach to see if she might detect a flash of skin if his cargo shorts slipped down on his hips, but no dice. "I didn't. I was just out for a run with my mom when we saw you."

"Aw, running with your mom," Sawyer said jokingly. "That's adorable."

Marnie could feel herself blushing and didn't want

Sawyer to see, so she decided to do something bold yet harmless and grabbed Sawyer's hat off his head. "Not as adorable as this Little League cap," she said, and ran away.

Sawyer left his skateboard behind and chased her down. "Give that back, Marnie!"

Even though she was still running from him, Marnie could tell from the pinched tone of Sawyer's voice that he was not amused by her antics. She halted in her tracks and spun around, expecting to hand over Sawyer's hat and apologize. But instead she broke into a laughing fit so enormous she nearly fell to her knees once again.

Half of Sawyer Lee's hair was shaved off his head!

"Wha-wha-what happened?" Marnie managed to spit out.

Sawyer scowled at her and snatched his hat from her hands. "Last night Brian Bennington got me back for the shoe polish on the binoculars stunt."

"Oh, no!" Marnie said, laughing harder.

"I appreciate your sympathy, thanks." Sawyer's lips broke into a half grin.

In fact, Marnie *was* sympathetic. She'd had a few painful encounters with a vengeful ex-friend recently and she hadn't ended up on top, either. After putting her hands on her hips and sucking in a deep breath, Marnie was able to regain part of her composure. "I'm sorry. You and your hair have my condolences."

Sawyer clamped the hat back on his head and smirked. "Yeah, yeah, yeah."

"So are you here plotting a way to settle the score?" she asked impishly.

"No, actually. I'm hiding from Zee," Sawyer replied, his smirk vanishing.

"Why?"

"I broke up with her yesterday," he answered.

Marnie felt as though someone had taken a glue gun to her ears. Even though things were dodgy between Sawyer and Lizette, she hadn't expected Sawyer to end things. Still, if this was true, why hadn't Lizette called her the minute it happened? Marnie had spent Saturday evening at home because Lizette had to meet her mother in the city for dinner, so she'd been around had her friend needed help getting through a breakup.

"Oh, my God, this is very . . . bizarre," she said, dumbfounded.

"Yeah, I know," Sawyer said as he sat down on his skateboard. "I didn't want to hurt her, Marnie." He glanced up at her and smiled a little. "But I couldn't go on pretending that I still liked her when . . . I don't."

There was definitely something about Sawyer's stare that made Marnie's heart skip close to forty-seven beats and her toes tingle.

"I should get going," she blurted out.

"Do you have to?" Sawyer leaped up. "Maybe I could teach you a few tricks on the board and then we could head over to the Chinese restaurant."

Marnie's eyes bulged.

Am I dreaming or is Sawyer asking me out ON A DATE?!?!

"Uh, I can't, I need to —"

"It's okay. I'll see you around sometime," Sawyer said simply as he hopped back on his skateboard and glided away.

When Marnie reached home after dragging her heels for a solid mile, she trudged up to her room and noticed that she had a text from Lizette on her cell phone.

CAN U IM ME? BOY DRAMA! ☹

Marnie flung herself face-first on her bed and pulled her pillow under her chin, thinking of how Lizette Levin's assessment of the current situation couldn't be more on the money.

Sunday, October 7, 10:17 A.M.

marniebird: *hey, zee*

queenzee: *hi, marn*

marniebird: *is everything ok?!?!*

queenzee: *ugh, i finally dumped sawyer*

marniebird: *what? really?*

queenzee: *yeah, he's such a himbo*

marniebird: *wow, i'm sorry*

queenzee: *don't B. i'm not!*

marniebird: *so r u moving on to ur secret crush . . . ?*

queenzee: *when r u going to learn? boyz come crawling 2 me ;-)*

marniebird: *LOL*

queenzee: *i'm sure there will B lots of hotties @ ur party on fri*

marniebird: *right, i'm SO psyched for it!*

queenzee: *me 2 ☺*

marniebird: *make DH 3*

queenzee: *aw, mr. romantic prob wants 2 do some pre-Homecoming snogging*

marniebird: *hahahaha, maybe ;-)*

queenzee: *ur so lucky 2 have him*

marniebird: *i know*

queenzee: *eep! brynne just got here, i should go*

marniebird: *oh, what are u 2 doing?*

queenzee: *nothing really*
marniebird: *well, can i come over? i'm bored out of my mind :-/*
queenzee: *maybe l8ter, i'll call u*
marniebird: *ok*
queenzee: *c ya!*
marniebird: *c ya*

Chapter 17

As soon as the bell for second period rang, Nola could tell that Monday morning's English class was already shaping up to be the preface to the apocalypse. When she entered the room, Nola felt someone shove past her so hard she nearly collided with the huge Shakespeare bust on the pedestal near the bulletin board. That certain someone was Marnie Fitzpatrick, who was without a doubt begging Nola to give her a triple-decker knuckle sandwich. Nola sneered at Marnie and pushed up the sleeves on her dark brown poplin jacket as though she was about to tear Marnie apart scrawny limb from scrawny limb.

"Hello, Pinocchio."

Nola looked over her right shoulder and saw Weston smirking at her as if he'd just spouted the most hilarious joke ever. She rolled her eyes and walked over to her desk, taking notice of how Marnie scowled at her and Weston when they passed by.

"Oh, c'mon. Aren't you going to tell me another ridiculous story? I really want to see your nose grow," Weston said, and took his seat.

Nola flopped down in her chair and didn't turn around. On Friday, Mr. Quinn had assigned the desk behind her to Mr. Baseball Fever, and she had a feeling this was instant karma for pulling the proverbial wool over Weston's pitifully stupid eyes. Nevertheless, Nola didn't regret what she'd done to Weston or Marnie, especially now that her arm might be broken.

"Attention, class," Mr. Quinn called out from the front of the room. When Nola's fellow students didn't comply right away, he put two fingers in his mouth and whistled loud enough that Principal Baxter probably heard him from the other end of the hall.

"That's better," Mr. Quinn continued when everyone was quiet. "As most have you noticed, a new student was added to our roster on Friday. I didn't have the chance to properly introduce him, so I thought I'd take a minute to do so now. Weston, could you come up here, please?"

Nola glanced over at Marnie as Weston strode down the aisle with his usual arrogant strut. She giggled when she saw how Marnie sighed and buried her head in her hands. As much as Weston annoyed Nola, his move back to Poughkeepsie couldn't have been better timed.

"Class, this is Weston Briggs," Mr. Quinn announced while Weston blew a big bubble and cracked it with his tongue. "He is an all-star athlete with a fabulous academic record. In fact, last year, he was the only one at Mortimer Academy with straight A's."

Nola gulped as Weston raised his eyebrows at her. *Straight A's?* Did that mean Weston was smarter than his jockstrap? Or was he an even bigger con artist than Nola was these days?

"Would you care to tell us more about yourself, Weston?" Mr. Quinn asked, gesturing to the crowd of people who seemed to be very interested in this Greek god–looking simpleton all of a sudden.

"I'd love to," Weston said, flashing everyone a bright, flawless smile. "I'm fourteen years old. My favorite baseball team is the Boston Red Sox. And I used to make out with Marnie Fitzpatrick in the shed behind her house."

As the class started snickering, Nola turned toward Marnie to see how her ex-best friend was dealing with this spontaneous and hilarious outburst from Weston. Marnie had succumbed to the humiliation, all right. Her head was now facedown on her desk and she had just pulled up the hood of her bright pink Juicy sweatshirt.

Holy crap! Weston is my hero!

"That will do, Mr. Briggs," Mr. Quinn said. The nasal tone indicated his displeasure.

Nola leaned back in her chair smugly. She had Weston pegged all wrong. Not only was he more intelligent than she'd originally thought, but he also possessed a true knack for making Marnie squirm.

"One more thing," Weston piped up before blowing another small bubble and cracking it. "When Nola James was in the seventh grade, she threw up on the Scrambler at the county fair, and her mom had to drive over and bring her a change of clothes."

While everyone around her started laughing, Nola slunk so low in her seat that she could barely see over her open textbook. There was only one other person in the world who knew about the Puke-ucular Crisis of 2006, and she hadn't lifted her head from her desk. Nola gingerly scooted up and peeked at a self-satisfied-looking Weston — sure, she had some dirt on him via Marnie "'zip my lips' is just a figure of speech" Fitzpatrick, but now that Nola had witnessed just how clever and sharp Weston was, going after him would be like covering her body in honey and cracking her brothers' ant farm open — not wise.

Mr. Quinn silenced the class again with an eardrum-piercing whistle and ordered Weston back to his desk. Weston tipped his baseball hat to him, sauntered toward a dumbstruck Nola, and returned to his assigned seat.

"Two can play at your game," Nola heard Weston whisper as Mr. Quinn began his lecture, and Marnie remained motionless in her chair.

Nola remembered how she'd threatened to spill all

her friend-turned-enemy's secrets on Friday, but that was before she was aware that Marnie had spilled more than one of her secrets to Weston a long time ago. But how much did Weston really know? And what would she have to do to convince him to keep his mouth shut?

Even Nola 2.0 was afraid to find out.

Nola squandered three dollars and fifty cents on her lunch, which consisted of crinkle fries, a carton of chocolate milk, and two oatmeal raisin cookies. She didn't even care if her mom smelled all the additives on her breath when she came home from work. The only way Nola could get through the rest of this crappy day was to gorge herself on carbs and sugar.

When she sat down in between Iris and Evan at their regular table, Iris gaped at the items on Nola's tray and made a sickened face.

"Does anyone know the number of the colon abuse hotline?" Iris asked, taking a sip of the glass noodle soup she had brought from home.

"I need comfort food," Nola muttered as she mindlessly yanked the ketchup out of Evan's hand and squeezed it over her fries. Only when she looked up at Evan and saw him grinning did she notice her bad manners. "Sorry, Ian."

Evan squinted at Nola and crossed his arms over his chest. "Who's Ian?"

Oh, good Lord.

Nola didn't even bother glancing over to Iris. She knew the girl must have a wily, told-you-so smile plastered all over her face.

"Yes, Nola. Tell us about this Ian fellow," Iris said in a mocking tone.

Nola shifted her gaze back to her plate and started shoveling fries into her mouth two at time so that when she spoke, her words were a jumbled, incomprehensible mess. She was aware of the choking risk but was actually hoping a fry might get caught in her throat. That way, she'd die and wouldn't have to look at Iris again.

"When did Nola turn into that speech-challenged kid on *Fat Albert*?"

Nola's head shot up and her eyes brightened at the sound of that familiar voice. She was smiling so hard that her cheeks were bulging like a squirrel that had eaten too many acorns. In any other company, Nola would probably get embarrassed and hive-ridden, but now that Matt was across from her, she felt more at ease and relaxed than she had in days.

"Welcome back, bonehead," Iris said with a shake of her bangs.

"Aw, Iris, you're such a sweetie," Matt said as he performed some silly handshake with Evan.

"When did you get into town?" Nola managed to say after she swallowed her food.

"Late last night," Matt said with an exhausted sigh. "I slept in, but I'm still beat."

Nola could tell by the discoloration underneath Matt's eyes that he hadn't been getting enough rest, wherever he'd been.

"So did anything interesting happen while I was gone?" Matt asked while picking a French fry off of Nola's plate. Nola almost laughed when she thought about the level of hijinks that ensued over the course of Matt's absence, but then a shiver of fear rushed over her once she heard him say, "I'm in the mood for gossip."

Oh . . . God . . . NO! What if Evan tells Matt about the ridiculous rumor Marnie tried to start about us? That might be worse than CHOKING TO DEATH!

"No, not really," Evan replied, toying with the straw in his carton of Tropicana.

Nola exhaled in relief. At least she was safe for now.

"What, did you think the school would burn down or something because you weren't here?" Iris said as she slurped her soup.

Matt laughed. "Actually, I was expecting a ticker tape parade upon my return. You guys are such slackers."

"Um, I thought I was a *whacker*," Evan chuckled.

Iris wiped her mouth with the back of her hand. "Oh, those labels are *so* September, Sanders. Try to keep up with the rest of us, will you?"

"See ya later," Evan mumbled, and got up from the table, taking his tray with him.

"Evan is way too sensitive," Iris said. "Just like you, Nola."

Nola shrugged. She wasn't even going to attempt to verbally spar with debate team phenom Iris.

"C'mon, Nola isn't *that* sensitive," Matt said dismissively.

Nola was going to shrug again but realized he had kind of insulted her just then. Still, she decided to let it slide. Matt was obviously run-down, and that could put anybody — even someone as nice as him — on edge.

"What are you talking about? When I was over at her house, she cried because she lost at *Scene It*," Iris argued. "Twice!"

Nola gripped her fork tightly, willing herself not to stab Iris in the arm. "I told you, there was *something* in my *eye*."

"Excuses, excuses," Matt said to Nola. "That's all I hear out of you lately."

Forget Iris. Now Nola wanted to fork Matt in the arm. Why was he picking on her like this? Because she didn't drop everything to talk to him the other day, like she *always* did? Matt hadn't even bothered to tell her what was so important that he'd taken off with his dad and missed school, let alone any other details that would shed light on his shady past. How could he be so hypocritical?

A Mariah Carey tune (circa *The Emancipation of Mimi*) rang out from Iris's cell phone, which was lying next to her soup. She checked out the caller ID and grinned mischievously.

"I gotta split," she said, quickly leaving the table and the remnants of her lunch behind her.

Nola gulped.

Now it's just . . . us.

Matt rubbed his temples and yawned. "I thought she'd never leave us alone."

It surprised Nola how one sentence from Matt could make her let go of her fork and any brief surge of anger she had toward him.

"Sorry if I'm acting like a jerk, I'm just . . . upset," he added.

Nola didn't know what to say. Asking Matt what was wrong never seemed to work, so instead she just handed him one of her oatmeal raisin cookies. "Will this cheer you up?"

"Yes, it will," Matt said, smiling. He took the cookie

out of Nola's grasp, grazing his thumb over her palm. After he bit into the cookie, he started laughing. "I'm glad you finally decided to trust the Quakers."

"Me, too." Nola could feel her cheeks turning pink at Matt's inside joke. The thought of him remembering the moment they shared in her kitchen together after the rainstorm made her heart swell with happiness.

"Listen, I feel bad about that call I made on Saturday."

Nola raised her eyebrows. "You do?"

"I'd just gotten off the phone with Riley and I was in a horrible mood," Matt explained.

Nola was concerned that her eyebrows were touching her hairline now, but there wasn't much she could do about it. "Why is that?"

"Well," Matt shifted nervously in his seat, "she was sort of mad that you didn't reply to her e-mail."

"Oh."

"Don't you like her?" Matt asked.

More like I hate her.

"I was just too busy to write her back, that's all," Nola said softly. She sensed that Riley hadn't revealed the contents of her e-mail to Matt, but she knew that ratting Riley out would just put additional stress on his shoulders. And telling him that she hoped Riley caught a bad case of dysentery wouldn't ease his troubles, either. So lying seemed like the right thing to do, even though it made Nola wince.

"Well, I'd appreciate it if you would," Matt said, scratching the back of his neck. "It would take some of the heat off me."

"What do you mean?"

He rolled his eyes. "Riley's a great girl, but she can be . . . delusional sometimes. I think she believes that . . . you *like* me or something."

Nola chugged all of her chocolate milk, praying the small amount of caffeine from the cocoa would prevent her from losing consciousness.

"I told Rye we were just friends and not to worry, but I think she'd feel better if you weren't such a mystery to her, know what I mean?"

Oh, I know what you mean.

"Anyway, it would be great if you could be, like, cyber pen-pals with her, just until things settle down," Matt said, finishing off his oatmeal raisin cookie. "That okay?"

Nola took her hand and pressed down on her empty milk carton, flattening it in one quick motion. Why was Matt always asking her for inane favors when it came to Riley? Make her a freaking "Welcome to Poughkeepsie" necklace. E-mail her so she won't be such an insecure moron. *Come on!* Enough was enough.

Still, when Nola stared deep into Matt's weary but glimmering hazel eyes, she couldn't possibly deny him anything. So she nodded in agreement. Yet as Matt thanked her and kissed one of her pink cheeks, the only person Nola wanted to stab with her fork was herself.

Chapter 18

THINGS TO REMEMBER DURING FIRST OFFICIAL
STUDENT COUNCIL MEETING

1) Suggest holding a car wash or a raffle to raise money for Homecoming dance decorations.

2) Sit up straight and don't slouch — posture is key to exuding authority!

3) Try not to blush every time Dane looks at me. (Is this even possible?)

4) Thinking about the following is absolutely, definitely prohibited!

   a) Sawyer breaking up with Zee and then kinda-sorta asking me out. How crazy weird is that?!

   b) Zee saying she broke up with Sawyer when she didn't — or did she? I don't know who to believe anymore.

   c) Giving that English presentation with Nola this week. Ugh, I still can't believe I have to even breathe the same oxygen as her!

   d) Weston Briggs and his big fat mouth.

   e) Why Zee didn't call me yesterday or invite me to hang out like she'd said she would — something is fishy.

   f) And that fish is probably none other than the gap-toothed demon! Grrr!

On late Monday afternoon, Marnie sat in the third row of lecture hall 4 with her shoulders back and her head held high. Since this was her first student council meeting as freshman class treasurer, she knew how important it was to appear unshakable and self-assured. Given the weekend and day she'd had, that wasn't an easy task.

As each one of her fellow civic-minded classmates filed in, Marnie's stomach twitched nervously. Sure, she'd traded in her Juicy sweatshirt and flare-leg cords for a killer outfit that would stun any Majors into submission — a silver metallic balloon-sleeved top from bebe, a black stretch-cotton pencil skirt with a ruffle hem, and lace-up calf-high boots — but that wasn't going to stop her from dwelling on all the commotion in her life. Even though she was still staring at the long list of things to remember during this meeting, Marnie was having trouble wiping the slate clean in her head, especially when it came to . . .

"Is this seat saved?"

Marnie turned her head and saw two hands partly tucked in a pair of jeans pockets. Her eyes slowly scanned the rest of this boy's body from the waist up. First, there was the loose-fitting baseball jersey; then, the broad shoulders; next, the deliciously smooth neck; after that, the most chiseled jawline on the eastern seaboard;

followed by the softest lips Marnie had ever kissed (which, thanks to him, everyone at Poughkeepsie Central knew about by now); and finally, the most vacant brown eyes she had ever stared into.

"Yes, Weston, it is," Marnie said gruffly. "Actually, this whole row is saved *for my friends.*"

Weston took his hands out of his pockets and folded the brim of his hat nonchalantly. "Well, since we're *Best Buddies,* I guess that means I can sit here, too."

Marnie kept her gaze fixed on the front of the room. "We are *not* buddies."

Even though her jerk of an ex had made an ass out of her this morning, she couldn't afford to let him get under her skin. In a few minutes, Marnie would be called on to address the group about the freshman class's financial contribution to the Homecoming dance, and while Dane had coached her through her short presentation on Saturday, she knew that acting poised was all up to her.

Still, it wouldn't feel like "acting" if the strange things that had taken place in the last forty-eight hours hadn't happened. All of a sudden, Marnie felt like someone had taped a "Serve Me Good" sign on her back. And with Weston blabbing about their hot-and-heavy eighth-grade kissing sessions, she was concerned that her privacy and image might be in jeopardy.

"Mmmm, you smell really good," Weston said after leaning toward Marnie and sniffing. "Better than I remember, in fact."

"God, Weston, can't you tell that I'm ignoring you?"

"If that's true, then why are you talking to me?" he asked coyly.

Marnie turned and peered at the grimace on Weston's face. If someone had told her when they broke up that he'd come back to torture her like this, she would have begged her mom and dad to send her to a remote part of the country where she could live out the rest of her life as a zany forest hermit.

"Well, I *won't* be talking to you from now on, *okay*?" she snapped.

"I doubt Mrs. Roberston would think that's a good idea, considering our little arrangement."

Marnie felt everything from her elbows to her chin get blazing hot. Amid all the drama, she had completely forgotten that she'd agreed to take Weston under her wing, so to speak. Still, that didn't mean that Marnie had to be nice to him, did it?

"Well, consider *this*. Tell anyone else anything else about our private business and I will see to it that you are sufficiently ruined, got that?"

"Wow, I had no clue you were this feisty!" Weston appeared very cocky and lecherous, but Marnie wasn't surprised. He looked that way 95 percent of the time when he wasn't playing, watching, or talking about baseball.

Marnie was about to feisty him upside the head when she detected the scent of sulfur in the air. Which could only mean one thing.

The devil's spawn was in striking distance.

Marnie's eyes darted toward the door and sure enough, there stood Brynne Callaway, clad in a pair of stacked-heel Chloé pumps and a cleavage-enhancing sweater that just screamed, "Hi, I'm an attention-seeking bimbo! It's a pleasure to meet you!" Although there were about ten empty seats scattered throughout the room, Brynne didn't waste a second surveying the area and picking the spot where she could do the most damage. Marnie dug her manicured nails into her palms as she watched Brynne's nasty glare take form.

Okay, Marnie, get ready for this nitwit. And don't back off, either!

"Hey, Wes," Brynne said, simpering.

Unfortunately, Marnie had witnessed Brynne and Weston flirting in homeroom this morning and it seemed like she was going to watch a repeat performance.

Oh, puh-lease.

"Hi, Brynne," Weston replied as he silently challenged Brynne's chest to a stare-down. "Have a seat."

At first, Brynne shot Marnie a heinous glare, but then she parked herself next to Weston, anyway, and smiled. "Omigod, your hat is *so boss*," she cooed.

"Thanks," Weston said, still hawkin' Brynne's goods.

Marnie rolled her eyes. Regardless of the size of her rack, Brynne could never be Lizette in a million years, no matter how hard she tried. Speaking of which, Lizette should have been here by now; the meeting was going to start any second. Marnie picked her butt up off her seat and looked around the lecture hall quickly. She noticed Jeremy Atwood, who was co-homeroom rep with Lizette, sitting in the front row (predictably), but her friend was still MIA.

"Looking for someone?" Weston had managed to pull himself away from Brynne's twins for a brief moment.

"Just Lizette," Marnie answered.

"Oh, Zee and Dane took off after school," Brynne said with a heaping dose of haughtiness.

Marnie was sure her nails had penetrated her skin and hit some nerve endings because she couldn't feel a thing.

"Guess us homeroom reps will have to take notes for them, right, Weston?"

Marnie's stomach twitches instantly transformed into a category 5 storm of spasms. How could Lizette and Dane ditch her on such an important day? Both of them knew that she was making her first real student council speech at this meeting, and she'd told them during lunch about this morning's hellish English class. Neither one of them had indicated that they wouldn't be around to lend their support, and Marnie definitely didn't remember hearing them say that they'd had plans *together*. Marnie tried to remind herself not to doubt either of them like she had in the past, but Dane had already asked her to the dance, so he didn't need Lizette's help wooing her anymore. What could they possibly be up to?

The infinite possibilities had Marnie so rattled that she didn't even realize that the meeting had begun. Thankfully, she shook herself out of her stupor and got her bearings as soon as senior class president Stephen Gustafson said, "And now, freshman treasurer Marnie Fitzpatrick will talk about her class's monetary donation to the Homecoming dance fund."

Marnie got up slowly, clasping her note cards tightly as though they had the power to roll back the wheels of time to when Lizette nominated her for freshman class treasurer, so that she could respectfully decline. Or perhaps just back to lunch so she could have fasted instead of eating two hot dogs with sauerkraut. Once Marnie got up to the podium, she took a deep breath and stared out into the sea of people, hoping that the sickening thought of Lizette and Dane sneaking off somewhere in his father's Jag would disappear long enough so that she could wow her audience with her fund-raising plans. But when she saw Brynne Callaway twirling a familiar-looking purple marker in her fingers, every single one of Marnie's well-plotted words got caught in her throat.

As her heart raced out of control, Marnie did her best to calm down and read the bullet points that were listed on her note cards. However, when it became clear that Brynne intended to goad Marnie into a slugfest in front of a room full of Leeks and Majors, her nerves got the better of her. The only thing Marnie could bring herself to do under the circumstances was blurt out, "I think we should have a car wash. More on that later. Thanks!" Then she bolted out of the lecture hall doors and dashed to the ladies' room, where she took cover in one of the stalls.

Marnie was sitting on the toilet and breathing rapidly as she ran through the last few minutes in her head — having to put up with Weston and his crap, hearing that Lizette and Dane had skipped the meeting so they could hang out together, seeing Brynne twirl that marker around with that sinister smirk of hers. It had been way too much for her to handle. But her heart almost handed in its letter of resignation to her circulatory system when she heard someone else walk into the bathroom. Marnie glanced down to the bottom of the stall door and saw a pair of Chloé pumps appear.

"Did you need to readjust your thong?"

Without thinking about what might happen next, Marnie slammed her hands against the stall door so that it swung open and nearly nailed Brynne in the nose. "No, but I may need to readjust your face *with my fists*!"

Brynne backed up a little and leered at her. "Spare me, Marnie. You don't have the guts."

"Did it take a lot of guts to *wreck my posters*?" Marnie asked, her rigid stance menacing.

"Not really," Brynne replied snottily. "I had help."

Marnie couldn't believe that Brynne had just admitted to destroying her posters *and* having an accomplice. Just as she suspected, Nola had been in on this all along. "I'm turning you and Nola in to Principal Baxter the first chance I get."

Brynne chuckled as she picked the flaking polish off one of her nails. "You must be joking. I don't *ever* associate with freaks like Nola James. Even when it benefits me."

Marnie was totally confused. If Nola hadn't been working with Brynne, then who had?

"And if you tell Principal Baxter, then I'll tell Zee that you were with Sawyer at the skate park on Sunday," Brynne said as she spun around and admired herself in the mirror.

Marnie cracked her knuckles loudly. "Do you have someone *following me*?"

"Maybe I do." Brynne ran her fingers through her hair and blew her reflection a kiss. "And maybe they are telling me things that you wouldn't want getting back to Zee."

"Like what?"

"Like how you are fooling around with her ex."

"I'm *not* fooling around with Sawyer," Marnie snarled.

Brynne turned back around and shrugged at Marnie. "That's not what my spy says."

"Well, your spy is dead wrong."

"I have to say, my source hasn't been wrong yet. Just look at how accurate the "Thong Thief" info was." Brynne's voice was cheery, like she was about to watch someone pelt Marnie with two tons of garbage. She put her hand on her hips and tilted her head, a pose that models and celebrities like to rock on the red carpet. "I better get back to the meeting. See ya, loser!"

Once Brynne strutted out of the bathroom, Marnie went to the sink and splashed some tepid water on her hot face. She grabbed a couple of paper towels and blotted her cheeks and forehead, then glanced at herself in the mirror. While Marnie was surprised to see that her waterproof mascara had held up, the bigger surprise here was that she'd never wanted to talk to Nola more.

Chapter 19

Nola's favorite part of the school week was her Tuesday afternoon study hall in Poughkeepsie Central's sprawling library. She had slipped into this routine where she'd weave through the stacks and run her fingers over the book spines. Sometimes a hint of gold foil print or the uniqueness of the author's last name would catch her eye and she'd pull out the book, flip open to a random section, and stand there reading it until she heard the bell ring. Nola looked forward to this time alone, and since this particular study hall group wasn't very big, the librarians let her wander around aimlessly as much as she wanted.

But today Nola was stuck at a table with Evan Sanders, preparing their portion of the group oral report they had to give in English class. Although Nola and Evan had hung out at the same lunch table every day and were thrown into this Helen Keller mess, she didn't really know too much about him, aside from the fact that he was addicted to electronic devices and liked her Chex party mix recipe.

As Nola glanced up from her notebook, she watched Evan furiously typing up their script on his laptop, his fingers dancing around the keyboard while his eyes stayed glued to the screen. She wondered what possessed him to pipe up when Marnie was trying to spread that lame-ass rumor about her and Matt mixing it up in Deirdre Boyd's closet. Like Nola, Evan was soft-spoken and seemed content with standing in other people's shadows, which is why his actions didn't quite make sense. Nola's best guess was that Evan defended her because he didn't want his friend to get burned — Matt was already knee-deep in an intense, albeit secret, personal turmoil and didn't need to deal with stupid crap at school. What other reason could there have been?

Nola couldn't come up with one, but either way, she felt like she owed Evan some gratitude for coming to her aid. She also wanted to ensure he would continue to stomp out the rumor if it did happen to circulate farther than their little English class group.

If only I could just do it without looking like an idiot.

"So maybe you should talk about the life and times of Louis Braille, and I should talk about the invention and production of the books," Evan said, his voice low.

She nodded. "Sounds good."

He glanced at Nola over the screen of his Mac and then averted his eyes once they met hers. "I can whip up some graphics with PowerPoint if you want."

"Sure."

Evan hit a few more buttons and closed his laptop while Nola wrote some additional details about Louis Braille in her notebook. When she was finished, she set her KISS pencil down and checked the clock on the wall. There were just five minutes left in study hall, and Evan had already grabbed his Sidekick out of his bag. If she didn't thank him soon, Nola might lose her chance. Then she'd have to summon up her courage and get into antihive mode all over again.

Nola cleared her throat but Evan was trapped in a Sidekick trance. She tried a second time and added a cough, but no reaction from Evan. Frustrated, Nola tore out a piece of scrap paper from her notebook, balled it up, and tossed it at Evan. However, her aim was off and it sailed over his right shoulder, landing on the floor. She had no choice but to snap him out of it the old-fashioned way.

"AHEM!" Nola said loudly.

It caught Evan so completely off guard that he dropped his Sidekick. The rest of their study hall cohorts looked over at them curiously. When a shrill "Shhhhh!" came from behind the librarian's desk, Nola covered her face in embarrassment.

"What is it?" Evan whispered. His cheeks were flushed.

"Sorry, I . . . I just wanted to say thanks for sticking

up for me the other day," Nola whispered back as she scratched a bump forming near her collarbone.

Evan smiled as his cheeks flushed an even darker shade of pink. "No problem."

"I really owe you one," she said.

"Actually, you did fine on your own. I thought Marnie was going to faint when you told her off."

Nola grinned when she recalled that satisfying moment. "Yeah, well, if you hadn't called Marnie out on that lie, Sally might have spread it to the entire student body."

"I wouldn't count Sally out just yet," Evan mumbled as his smile faded.

"What do you mean?"

"Sally asked me yesterday if I had any solid proof that Marnie was making that story up and . . . well, I said No," he explained, the corners of his mouth turning down even farther.

Nola could feel her soul being sucked out of her body. "Why did you say *No*?!"

Another "SHHHHHHH!!!" bellowed out from the librarian.

"Because I don't." Suddenly, Evan was a ball of nervous energy. He looked like a frightened kitten that wanted to scamper away.

"Why did you say anything at all then?"

"Well, I knew it wasn't true because Matt would never . . ." he trailed off.

"Never what?"

Be caught dead kissing me?? Is that it?

"Never mind," Evan murmured as he grabbed his laptop and bolted out the library door faster than a speedboat, leaving Nola to rock in his choppy wake.

marniebird: *hey, r u busy?*

erinfitzparty: *kind of, getting ready 2 go out*

marniebird: *i just need ur advice on something*

erinfitzparty: *ok, but make it fast, cal is on his way over*

marniebird: *well, u remember lizette levin, right?*

erinfitzparty: *yes, rachel's cuz, what about her?*

marniebird: *she and i have been hanging out a lot*

erinfitzparty: *good! maybe now u'll live up to my rep*

marniebird: *whatev*

marniebird: *anyway, her friend brynne is like, harassing me, and i don't know what 2 do*

erinfitzparty: *this is easy, u just suck it up*

marniebird: *that's all u have 2 say?*

erinfitzparty: *yeah, what else is there?*

marniebird: *maybe i'll just tell LL*

erinfitzparty: *then u'll look like a whiny little girl who can't deal*

marniebird: *but brynne also threatened to tell LL that I am messing around with LL's ex bf*

erinfitzparty: *well, r u?*

marniebird: *no! of course not!*

erinfitzparty: *chill, marn. it happens to the best of us, u know*

marniebird: *um, I guess so*

erinfitzparty*: in that case, i'd get down on my knees and* *beg this brynne girl, kiss her ass, do whatever it takes to make sure she doesn't rat u out to LL*

marniebird: *but i didn't even do anything wrong!*

erinfitzparty: *doesn't matter, sis. it's all going to come down to ur word against hers, and LL will choose her, mark my words*

marniebird: *that's not true, LL is def closer 2 me these days, half the time LL acts like she can't even stand brynne*

erinfitzparty: *u r the new member of the group, marn, the 1 most easily replaced, regardless of LL's yo-yo relationship with brynne*

marniebird: *i C*

erinfitzparty: *get ready 2 pucker up, buttercup ;-)*

marniebird: *ha-ha, v. funny*

erinfitzparty: *can I go now?*

marniebird: *yes, bye*

erinfitzparty: *good luck, ur gonna need it*

Chapter 20

On Wednesday night, Marnie's mom dropped her off in front of Grier Hopkins's house near Locust Grove. She and the girls were going to practice sneaking over to the mansion so that they wouldn't mess up, come Friday night. As Marnie walked up the brick-lined driveway and along the wood-chip-covered path that led to the back of Grier's enormous palacelike abode, she knew that she should be feeling ecstatic. In two days, she would be the brilliant star of the best shindig of the fall season. The most awesome guy at Poughkeepsie Central and the VP of the sophomore class would be on her arm at the Homecoming dance in a few short weeks. Her closest friend was worshipped and adored by kids in Dutchess *and* New York counties. What more could she want?

But when Marnie opened the white picket-fence door and came across her friends swimming in Grier's oasis of a heated swimming pool, the answer to that question became oh so clear.

That Brynne Callaway would get a cramp in her side and drown.

"Took you long enough to get here," Lizette said

playfully as she treaded water in the deep end and splashed Marnie's silver flip-flop-clad feet.

"I couldn't find my bathing suit," Marnie said, tugging on the drawstrings of her white terry-cloth cover-up skirt.

"Lame excuse!" Lizette said, splashing her again.

Marnie half grinned. Speaking of lame excuses, Lizette had explained that she and Dane missed the student council meeting yesterday because she'd gotten a D on her math test and needed an emergency yoga session to unwind. Apparently, Mr. Levin couldn't come to pick Lizette up and when she saw Dane getting some items out of his car, she begged him to give her a ride over. It sounded innocent enough, but Marnie still couldn't help but feel jealous, even though she wanted to cling to the memory of her date with Dane like an anti-envy blanket.

The truth was she just couldn't make sense of Lizette lately. One minute she'd be so supportive and pro-Marnie, the next she'd be sidling up to Brynne or interfering with Dane. As she stood there, noticing how Lizette's makeup was perfect even in the water, Marnie remembered a time not too long ago when she would have opened her heart to Nola without hesitation or fear of rejection. And after she learned that Nola wasn't involved in the posters scandal, Marnie found herself reminiscing about their friendship a lot more than she wanted to.

But walking down memory lane would be a huge mistake now. It would only distract Marnie from more important matters, like making sure Brynne didn't sink her battleship.

Grier waved to Marnie from the top of the pool slide. "Come on in, Marn. The water is nice and warm!" She adjusted the tie on her pink halter-top swimsuit and slid down the slide with her arms in the air. The splash was gigantic and sprayed everything within a ten-foot radius, including Brynne, who was sitting on the edge of the pool, dangling her long legs in.

"God, Grier! I told you I didn't want to get my hair wet!" Brynne shouted as she patted her bangs with her hands.

"Don't spaz, Brynne. It's just a little chlorine." Lizette swam to the ladder and climbed up, revealing her dazzling supermodel body and her mismatched bikini — a tiny red string top with little blue anchors on it, and a yellow-and-purple-polka-dot bottom. Marnie ran her hand over her tummy at the sight of Lizette's firm stomach and reminded herself to lay off the Fiddle Faddle.

"Zee, you know how frizzy my hair gets in these

conditions," Brynne whined, tugging on a damp strand with her finger. "I need a towel."

Marnie realized instantly that this was her cue to perform the gruesome task her big sister, Erin, suggested in their IM chat. Even though it was going to kill her pride and crush her soul, Marnie knew it had to be done so that she could maintain order in her delicate, fragile, yet totally stellar social universe.

Oh, God, here I go.

"I'll get it, Brynne," Marnie chirped. She dropped her straw beach bag with her change of clothes on the damp, tiled floor and jogged over to the lounge chair stacked with fluffy green towels. Marnie grabbed one from the top of the pile and dashed back over to Brynne with her arm stretched out.

Brynne looked down at the towel in Marnie's hand as though she had just cleaned a sewer pipe with it. "I don't like this one."

Marnie clutched the towel tightly. "Why not?"

"It doesn't seem thick enough," Brynne said, smirking evilly.

I'll show you thick, dog face!

Marnie gritted her teeth. "Fine, I'll go get another one." She stormed back over to the lounge chair, set the first towel on the ottoman, and picked up the next towel on the pile. Marnie presented it to Brynne without much fanfare.

Brynne took the towel out of Marnie's hand and then shook her head. "Um, this one isn't even fully dry."

The only thing keeping Marnie from blowing a gasket and murdering Brynne was that there'd be witnesses. "Actually, Brynne, I think you're mistaken."

"Are you saying I can't tell *wet* from *dry*?" Brynne asked, glaring at her.

Marnie's eyes drifted over to Lizette, who was doing handstands in the shallow end with Grier. It really amazed her how Lizette never seemed to be around when Brynne was attacking Marnie. Even so, Marnie gritted her teeth and bit the proverbial bullet.

"No, I'm not," she answered.

"Good. Then get me another one." Brynne tossed the towel right in Marnie's face.

Marnie grunted under her breath and walked back over to the lounge chair. There was only one more towel left and she was praying that Brynne would just take it and shut the hell up already. Marnie brought it back to Brynne and said, "Here."

Brynne barely inspected the towel this time, but she somehow managed to find something wrong. "There's a stain on it."

Marnie was starting to contemplate how many years

she'd have to serve in the clink if she smothered Brynne with this towel. Since she was a juvenile, she could be out in her mid-twenties. That wouldn't be too horrible.

"Brynne, there's no stain anywhere on this towel. It looks brand-new," Marnie said tersely.

"I think you should go inside and scrub that stain out," Brynne scoffed, then lowered her voice. "Unless you want Lizette to find out that you and Sawyer were knockin' boots."

Marnie couldn't believe that she was actually being blackmailed, and for what? Because Brynne saw Sawyer chasing her around at the skate park? Perhaps if Marnie told Lizette about it herself and explained that it was just harmless fun, Lizette wouldn't even care. Anyway, she was supposedly into another guy, and while some signs pointed to Dane in that scenario, Marnie chose not to think about that right now.

"Maybe I'll just call your bluff, Brynne. What do you say to that?" Marnie asked with a ruthless scowl on her face.

Brynne stood up real slow, like she was preparing to toss Marnie into the pool. Once she towered over Marnie, she placed her hands on her hips and pushed her intimidating and sizable chest out. "I say, bring it, Fatty."

"I'm sorry. Did you just call me *Fatty*?!"

"I'm sorry, are you deaf *and* fat?!"

That's it. This girl is worm food!

Marnie was about to lunge forward and tackle Brynne at the waist when Lizette and Grier appeared at their sides.

"So are you guys ready to go to the mansion?" Grier said as she took one of Brynne's discarded towels and wrapped it around her shoulders.

"I can't wait for your party, Marn. It's going to be boss!" Lizette pulled Marnie in for a wet hug.

Although Brynne looked as though she was going to hang Marnie from one of the trees in Grier's backyard, Marnie's demeanor softened the second Lizette let go. She marveled at how easy it was for Lizette to put her in a good mood, no matter what drama was going on.

"Let's get changed, okay? My mom will be home at eleven," Grier said.

"Lead the way," Marnie said as Lizette took her by the hand and pulled her along.

Fifteen minutes later, the girls were dressed in dark clothes and wearing their hair back in ponytails. Grier was ahead of the pack, pointing a flashlight down a tiny mulch-covered path off the back of her parents' yard while Lizette, Marnie, and Brynne followed close behind.

"Grier, I'm getting all these wood chips stuck in my shoes," Brynne whispered angrily.

"Will you shut up? You're going to get us caught," Lizette barked.

"We'll be there in a minute, guys. Just stay close," Grier advised as she wove through shrubbery so dense, Marnie could barely use her peripheral vision.

"I still don't see why we're doing this," Brynne said, her tone growing more and more furious with each step they took on the path.

Lizette heaved an annoyed sigh. "Duh! It's a secret-password party for a reason, Brynne. There has to be a surprise or else it's going to be whack. Get it?"

Marnie smiled so big the corners of her mouth hurt. Lizette's attitude about her party was definitely chipping away at the jealousy she felt over her getting a ride from Dane after school. And the fact that she was bickering with Brynne made Marnie overjoyed. In fact, Marnie couldn't think of any way this evening could get better, but then she came out from the tunnel of shrubbery and set foot in front of the Locust Grove mansion.

"Wow!" Lizette gasped when she feasted her eyes on the majestic structure.

Grier turned off her flashlight and grinned. "Isn't it *amazing* at night?"

"It's absolutely beautiful," Marnie said.

"Ugh, whatever. I'm going to sit on the steps," Brynne groaned.

With its porte cochere, two octagonal wings, and a four-story tower, the Tuscan-style house seemed enormous. The exterior was so immaculate that it must have appeared just as it had when the telegraph inventor, Samuel Morse, bought it back in 1847. While Marnie had seen the place before on a class field trip, it looked so new and fresh to her now. Maybe it was because spotlights were shining on the house, giving it an ethereal glow. Maybe it was because Lizette was going to great lengths to ensure her party would be legendary. Or maybe it was because Dane had mentioned that he couldn't wait to sneak out here with her.

"What are you thinking about?" Lizette said, nudging Marnie gently.

Marnie wondered if Lizette could see her blushing. "Oh, nothing."

"This place sure is bigger than the shed you're used to," Lizette said, nudging her again.

Now that Marnie's cheeks were white-hot she was positive Lizette would notice. "So you heard about me and Weston, huh?"

"What*ever*. You made out with a hottie! A lot of girls want to give you a medal," Lizette said, laughing.

The fact that Lizette commended Marnie on her past relationship with Weston immediately put her at ease.

"Well, what about you?" Marnie said, laughing a bit herself.

"What about me?"

"Are you *ever* going to dish about this new crush of yours?"

Marnie was hoping Lizette would confide in her, but instead she just giggled and said, "Eventually."

Marnie would have giggled, too, if Lizette hadn't darted off so she could sit on the steps with Brynne.

Chapter 21

to: *rf@rileyfinneganswake.com*
from: *nolaj1994@gmail.com*
subject: *Hi*

> *Riley,*
> *How are you?*
> *See ya,*
> *N*

Nola was hunched over her desk on Wednesday night, trying her best to write to Matt's girlfriend, Riley Finnegan. She'd been at it for about a half hour and all she had so show for it was this sorry excuse for an e-mail. Nola slumped over her keyboard and sighed. On the inside, she felt as though her emotions were out of control. It seemed to be getting worse every day and her temper was flaring up way more often than it used to. Last week, Nola had felt very powerful when she acted on her anger, but as she lay limp, her forehead pressing down on the F7 and F8 keys, she just felt empty.

Nola thought back to the summer, when she and Marnie had sunbathed on her deck or walked through the neighborhood underneath the light of a crescent moon. She was happy then, and it really scared Nola to think that the emptiness or anger would eventually swallow up each and every fragmented piece of joy that existed in her memory.

Nola sat up and wiped away the tears that were rolling down the sides of her nose. Then she pulled out a tissue from the pocket of her zip-up sweater and blew hard, just as someone knocked on her door. The last thing Nola wanted was a visit from Ian or the Terrible Twins, so she walked over to the door and said, "Go away!"

But the knocking was persistent.

Nola blotted her nose again with the tissue. "Leave me alone. I'm busy!"

Another *KNOCK-KNOCK-KNOCK.*

Nola rolled her eyes. "Do you need me to *sing* it to you?"

"Yes, please do," came a voice from the other side.

Is that who I think it is?

Nola opened the door. There stood Matt Heatherly, complete with his usual I-have-no-idea-you-love-me smile. And right behind him, of course, was Ian Capshaw, complete with his usual I'm-onto-you frown.

Oh, God. I think my eyes are bleeding.

Matt turned toward Ian, his hand outstretched. "Thanks, man. I can take it from here."

Ian shook Matt's hand hard. "Like Nola said, she's busy, so don't overstay your welcome."

"I won't." Matt rubbed his hand after Ian let go.

Ian shifted his gaze to Nola. "You need anything from downstairs? I have Dennis and Dylan in an hour-long time-out, so it's not a problem."

"I'm fine," she replied, lowering her eyes to the floor.

"Did you hear that, Ian? Nola said she's fine, so don't overstay your welcome." Matt stepped into Nola's room and shut the door in Ian's face.

Nola couldn't hold back her laughter. "You are too much."

"Are you kidding? Your bodyguard has me beat. What is his problem, anyway?"

Nola shrugged. All of sudden, talking with Matt about Ian seemed really . . . uncomfortable.

"Maybe he needs more fiber in his diet." Matt took a running leap onto Nola's bed and then sprawled out on his back.

"Our refrigerator is a fiber machine, so I don't think that's it."

Matt put his hands on his stomach and grinned. "Well, I do have another theory."

Nola stared at his black leather belt and the tarnished silver buckle as his tummy rose and fell with each breath. She stumbled over to her desk chair and sat down.

"What is it?" she asked.

Matt leaned up a little so he could see Nola's reaction. "This is just an educated guess, but I think he might . . . have a thing for you."

Nola spun around in her desk chair the second she felt a prickly sensation at the base of her neck. Out of all the awkward moments with Matt on record, this one certainly was in a league of its own.

"Um, I *seriously* doubt it," she muttered as she wistfully looked into Hannah's sparkling, two-dimensional eyes.

"Why is that so hard to believe?" Nola heard Matt say. "You're pretty, intelligent, artistic, and have a great sense of humor. There's a lot to like."

Nola's ears were burning up. She had longed for these words to come out of Matt's mouth for weeks now. But he wasn't even saying them on his own behalf, which made the emptiness Nola had felt earlier seem so much more overwhelming.

"Can we not talk about Ian's thing anymore?" Nola's voice was wavering a little, but once she realized that she'd just said "Ian's thing," she started giggling.

Matt chimed in with loud chuckles that forced Nola

to turn around. She absolutely loved the sound of his laugh, even now when it was obvious that while he saw all of her wonderful qualities, she would never be anything but a friend to him.

"Okay, fair enough," Matt said as he got up and moved to the edge of the bed so his knees were practically touching Nola's. "But like it or not, I came over here to talk to you in person about another *thing*. And I don't want you to freak out."

Oh, this ought to be good.

Nola gripped the arms of her chair. "What's wrong?"

"Nothing's wrong. It's just that . . . there's a certain rumor floating around about us."

Suddenly, Nola's fingernails were putting holes in the upholstery.

"I can explain. You see —"

"Evan already told me what happened with Marnie," Matt interrupted. "And it's not a big deal, really. There are worse *things* than people at school thinking I made out with a beautiful girl in a closet."

Nola blushed when she pictured her and Matt rolling around on the pile of dirty laundry in her own closet. There weren't too many things *better* than that, actually. "Thanks. For understanding, I mean."

"Hey, I'm a sensitive guy." Matt put his hand on her knee and squeezed it affectionately. "But there's more."

"There is?"

As long as it didn't have to do with Riley, Nola figured she could deal with whatever it was Matt was about to tell her. In fact, Nola was thrilled that Matt had come over here tonight to confide in her. Maybe she'd finally find out all the answers to her questions about him.

"Remember how I said it wasn't doubtful that someone would like you a lot?"

Hmmmm . . . this isn't where I was expecting our conversation to go.

"Duh, you said it just a minute ago," Nola said with an uneasy laugh.

"Yeah, well, Evan wanted to tell you himself, but he's even shier than you, if you can imagine that." Matt smirked. "Anyway, I agreed to play messenger."

"Wha . . . wha . . . *what*?" Nola stammered.

"Evan digs you, Nola. He has since the first day of school. That's why I asked you to sit down with us during lunch." Matt winked at her.

Nola wasn't sure, but she thought her feet might be swelling. Suddenly, her shoes felt so tight that she was afraid her toes might burst through the front of them. "I thought you were just being nice to me."

"Of course I was. I just meant that Evan is really eager to get to know you better, but when he didn't have the courage to say so, I told him I'd help him out," Matt explained. "Anyway, how cool would it be if two of my closest friends got together?"

How cool would it be? It would be the most uncool thing in the history of the universe! Nola wanted to reach over, grab Matt by the shirt, and shake him until he realized that she was crazy about *him*. But like Evan, Nola couldn't find the courage to tell Matt exactly how she felt. And at this point, she was wondering if she would ever get the courage.

"You know, Evan is a great guy," Matt said as he tapped Nola on the knee with his fist. "He's as smart as Bill Gates, so if you end up marrying him, you wouldn't have to work a day in your life."

Nola swore she felt her big toe break through the sole of her Skechers.

"And he's a hell of a dancer," Matt added. "Think of how handy that skill will come in at Homecoming."

"Wait a sec. Are you saying Evan is going to ask me to *Homecoming*?" Nola's voice was borderline shrill.

"I don't know for sure, but since he likes you so much, I think we can assume he will," Matt said. "What? You wouldn't want to go with him?"

As the rest of Nola's toes battled against the restrictive leather of her sneakers, she contemplated her answer. Here Matt was, telling her that Evan liked her, but not once did he ask Nola how she felt about Evan. Didn't that even matter? However, if Matt was so clueless that he couldn't see that Nola worshipped him just as Iris had observed, then maybe it didn't matter at all. In fact, maybe Nola should start dating Evan and go to the dance with him and smooch him all night long. Why not? Matt wasn't available or interested in her in the least.

"I . . . I'd go with him," Nola mumbled. "I guess."

"That's great!" Matt spun Nola around in her chair so hard she revolved five times.

When she finally came to a stop, Nola was facing her computer version of Hannah Montana, who was smiling like she'd never been in love with someone she couldn't have.

Chapter 22

On Thursday morning, Marnie fidgeted at her desk, wishing that English was an elective and not a required class. It was oral presentation day — a day that Marnie had been dreading since she got thrown into this gladiators' pit of an English project with her ex-best friend, who was currently fiddling with a laptop alongside Evan Sanders in the back of the room. Marnie had to admit, working privately with Sally Applebaum on the sign language portion of the project had brought her some much-needed stress relief, but now that she was only a few minutes away from standing (civilly, mind you) next to Nola in front of the entire class, she was really worried about the state of her blood pressure.

Then again, when Weston Briggs suddenly appeared and crouched down next to Marnie and her stiletto heels (on loan from Lizette), she was much more worried about the state of her sanity.

Weston turned his baseball hat backward and grinned at her. "You've been hard to track down, Buddy."

"Stop. Calling. Me. Buddy," Marnie said through gritted yet sparkling white teeth.

"Okay, Bud," Weston quipped.

Marnie rolled her eyes in disgust.

"So there's this rumor going around about a secret-password party this weekend. Do you know anything about it?" he asked.

Marnie's shoulders stiffened and the back of her bare knees began to sweat. There was no way in hell that Weston could be allowed into that party. Just the fact that he was in the same town as her was bad enough. If he even got into the vicinity of Grier's house, he would wreck the monumental evening she'd been looking forward to for weeks.

"No, I don't," Marnie said firmly.

"Really? Because you and your fancy, popular friends and your preppie boyfriend all seem to be in the know," Weston replied. "I'd hate to tell Mrs. Robertson that you were holding out and preventing me from becoming accustomed to life here at Poughkeepsie Central."

"Threatening me isn't going to get you an invite any faster," Marnie snapped.

"So there *is* a party!" Weston said, his face lighting up.

"Shhhhhh!" Marnie whispered. "Everyone will hear you."

"Where is it?" Weston muttered.

Marnie was a split second away from committing first-degree stiletto-stomping when Mr. Quinn bellowed out, "Take your seats, class. We're about to get started."

Weston stood up and smirked. "See you there, Bud."

Marnie grunted as he walked away, knowing that all too soon he'd be the least of her problems.

The first group of students who presented their Helen Keller project were so woefully unprepared that Mr. Quinn cut them off midway through and asked them nicely to stay after class. The second group, who performed a musical-inspired skit, fared a little better. The moment Mr. Quinn said, "Group three," Marnie's hands went ice-cold.

"You ready?" Sally said, tapping Marnie on the shoulder.

Marnie nodded her head and grabbed her notebook off of her desk. She got up, adjusted her low-rise Bitten jeans, strolled to the front of the room, and stood next to Sally. While Marnie plastered a confident albeit fake look on her face, she watched a cargo pants–clad Nola walk toward her, narrowing her eyes the closer she got to Marnie.

"Move. You're blocking the projection screen," Nola said tersely.

"Aye-aye, Captain," Marnie scoffed, and shifted her position an inch or two to the left.

"I said, *move*," Nola growled.

Marnie felt a very strong and potentially dangerous drop-kick vibe course through her body, but by some miracle, she held herself back. "I *did*."

"Why don't we just stand off to the side while Evan and Nola present first?" Sally certainly was a chip right off the diplomat's block.

"Fine," Marnie said with indignation. She and Sally relocated to the real estate next to the Shakespeare bust.

As Nola took her place at the front of the room, Marnie noticed that Nola's skin wasn't the slightest bit blotchy. In fact, Nola seemed rather calm and composed, which was quite astounding. Nola had broken out in hives while reciting a soliloquy from *Hamlet* in their eighth-grade drama class. That was just last year. How in the world had Nola become so strong and fearless?

And how did she do it without me? Marnie wondered.

Nola's composure wouldn't endure, though. Her speech was timed to the PowerPoint slides that Evan had made, and somehow they'd gotten out of order once Nola had run through the first two. Marnie watched as Nola dashed to where Evan was sitting behind his laptop, frantically trying to fix the technical glitch. Marnie was certain that everyone, including the Shakespeare bust, could see the red bumps forming on Nola's arms and neck.

Strangely enough, her first instinct wasn't to point and laugh at Nola, and considering the underhanded trick and nasty attitude Nola had subjected her to recently, Marnie believed Nola deserved it. However, as a flustered Nola and a panicked Evan struggled to get their act together, Marnie couldn't curb the desire to help Nola out of this embarrassing situation. Perhaps it was just one of those phantom limb–type experiences, which were impossible to ignore. Or perhaps it was a lot more complicated than that. Regardless of what the motivation was, Marnie swallowed hard, walked to the front of the room, and reached out to the girl who used to be her best friend.

"Hey, Nola. Why don't you come demonstrate this signing technique while Evan works on the PowerPoint problem?"

Nola looked at Marnie quizzically and then reluctantly joined her.

"Close your eyes and hold your hand with your palm facing out," Marnie instructed.

Nola gave her a sideways glance but followed Marnie's orders without argument.

Marnie began making the letters of the alphabet in sign language while pressing her hand into Nola's palm. "As most of you know, this is how Helen Keller learned how to communicate. It's a unique form of sign language used for those who are also blind."

Marnie glanced into the crowd and saw Mr. Quinn smiling with approval. She grinned in return, hoping that she'd saved their group grade along with Nola's butt.

"The slide show is back online," Evan piped up. The projection screen lit up again, much to his relief.

Immediately, Nola's eyes popped open and she ripped her hand away from Marnie. Without so much as a thank-you, Nola took a few steps forward and continued her part of the presentation with robotic-like precision. Marnie stood there dumbfounded for a moment, then slunk back to Sally and Shakespeare, cursing phantom limb–instincts and walks down memory lane, inside and out.

Marnie was an exhausted mess by the end of the day. As she gathered her belongings at her locker, she caught a glimpse of herself in her mirror and gasped in horror. Not only was her face extremely shiny and her pores clogged, but her hair had somehow become flat and greasy-looking. Marnie peered at her reflection even harder and saw a pink bump forming near the side of her nose. Definitely a zit. Marnie decided that her body's sudden increase of oil secretions could only be caused by intense stress. When Marnie tried to identify the source of that stress, she knew who was to blame.

Nola Freaking James.

Even though Marnie hadn't expected Nola to be all chipper and gracious after she saved Nola's part of their English class presentation from a colossal meltdown, her ungratefulness made her furious. Marnie had essentially gone out on a shaky limb for Nola and she just disregarded Marnie's martyrdom without even blinking an eye. Still, considering all of the complicated story lines that existed in Marnie's fairy-tale world, her ongoing war with Nola seemed like the conflict least likely to have a happy ending. As Marnie threw her social studies book into her tote bag, she reminded herself that things could always be worse.

"Hey, Marnie."

Up until a few days ago, Marnie really liked hearing Sawyer's voice, but now the sound of it made her feel as queasy as she had been when she went white-water rafting with her father early last summer. She didn't even bother to look at Sawyer, fearing that some spark might go off between them, and everyone in the hallway would see it.

"Hey," Marnie said minus any intonation. She

figured if she was blasé enough, he'd get bored and wander off.

Sawyer tapped his fingers on her locker door. "How are you?"

"Fine."

"That's good."

Ugh, why doesn't he get the hint?

"So, I hear you're going to the Homecoming dance with Dane."

Suddenly, Marnie felt as though all her joints were stiffening. She knew it shouldn't bother her that Sawyer had found out she was going to the dance with Dane, but it did. *A lot,* in fact.

God, this is SO twisted.

"Yeah, I am," Marnie replied nonchalantly.

"Too bad. I know somebody who wanted to ask you."

As soon as Sawyer said that, Marnie spun around to face him. However, the moment she saw his fully shaved head, she covered her mouth with both hands and laughed.

"Did Brian Bennington strike again?" Marnie asked through a chain of giggles.

Sawyer smiled. "No, I finished off his work. I *hate* wearing baseball hats."

That was music to Marnie's ears.

"Well, I like it," she said bashfully. And she wasn't lying. The super-short 'do made Sawyer's penetrating onyx-colored eyes seem even bigger and brighter. Not only that, but his jawline seemed more angular and defined. Without a doubt, Sawyer had taken his hotness to new heights, which would make avoiding him much more difficult.

"Oh, I can tell," Sawyer said with pretend arrogance. "Wanna rub my head?"

"No, thanks." It pained Marnie to utter those words. Passing up an invitation to touch Sawyer Lee was something only a nut job would do.

"Okay." Sawyer immediately made an about-face and started walking away.

Crap. Did I piss him off?

Given that Brynne had a spy out there somewhere, Marnie knew she shouldn't even be seen glancing in Sawyer's direction in public, let alone flirting with him, but she just didn't want him to leave feeling like she wasn't interested in rubbing his head. Because the truth was . . . Marnie was interested. More interested than she'd been since the moment she gave him the number one spot on her Crush List.

She had to go for it. *Had* to.

"Wait, you're not going to triple-dog dare me?" Marnie called out to him.

Sawyer turned back around and smirked. "I thought that line didn't work on you."

"Maybe it will this time."

What am I doing?

Sawyer walked ten paces toward Marnie and stopped no more than a few inches away from her, smiling like he was about to say something funny and adorable.

"I triple-dog dare you to rub my head, Marnie Fitzpatrick," Sawyer said, bowing down chivalrously so she wouldn't have to get on her tiptoes.

I repeat, WHAT AM I DOING?!?!

Marnie stood there perfectly still, trying to convince herself that this was an astronomically stupid idea and to back off right now or else reap the consequences. On the other hand, it was a *head rub*, for God's sake! There was nothing scandalous about it. The only reason she was behaving this cagey was because of Brynne and her threats. Was Marnie really going to let that evil wench intimidate her any more than she already had?

"What's going on here?"

Sawyer turned his head a little to the right. "Hey, Zee."

Oh, God, please let this be some sort of desert mirage.

Marnie slowly craned her neck to the left. Lizette stood there awkwardly in a brown-fringed, Pocahontas-inspired minidress and a pair of seersucker Tretorns, her arms crossed in front of her chest. She glared at Marnie like she'd had her tongue in Sawyer's mouth, while Grier lurked off to the side and gave Marnie a sympathetic look.

"I was just showing Marnie my new haircut," Sawyer explained as he ran his hand over the back of his head.

Lizette pursed her lips and her face became hard as nails. "I doubt Marnie cares. I know I don't."

Marnie was no idiot. She could tell by the fire in her friend's eyes that Sawyer had ditched Lizette and not the other way around.

Sawyer shook his head in bewilderment. "I think Marnie can speak for herself."

"Actually, I'd *love* to hear what Marnie has to say right now." Lizette zapped her with a frosty glare.

Marnie knew that this wasn't an ordinary loyalty test. This was a full-fledged "who do you love?" exam, which consisted of only one question — Sawyer or Lizette? If Marnie chose wrong, she'd have to say good-bye to everything she'd worked so hard for, and that seemed like way too much to risk, especially with Brynne on the loose. Although it did dawn on Marnie that Nola had never put this kind of pressure on her, this is what came with the Lizette territory, so she'd have to accept it or be kicked out of the Majors for good.

Marnie spun on her Lizette-loaner stiletto heels and faced Sawyer. "Honestly, you look like a yellow cue ball."

As Sawyer went into a daze, Lizette fell into Grier, doubled over in laughter. Marnie hadn't expected to blurt out something that harsh, but apparently she had passed the exam. Sawyer lowered his head and wandered off down the hall while Lizette threw her arm around her and squealed.

"Omigod, Marn! I think you made him cry!"

Thankfully, Marnie found a pair of oversized Jackie O–inspired shades in her bag and threw them on. Now Lizette wouldn't be able to tell that Marnie was crying, too.

Chapter 23

On Friday morning, Nola was engaged in a strange version of dodgeball, minus the actual ball. The object of the game was to avoid anyone Nola didn't want to look in the eye, and that list of people included Matt, Evan, Weston, Iris, and pretty much everyone else she knew. So far, she'd kept her nose buried in a copy of *The Age of Innocence,* thereby dodging Matt during homeroom. Weston almost brushed by her in the hallway, but she ducked behind a very tall freshman girl named Lydia and went virtually unnoticed.

As for Evan, Nola had managed to dodge him after English class, but it was no easy feat. When Nola had seen him walking toward her once Mr. Quinn dismissed them, she sprinted out the door so fast that she almost knocked the Shakespeare bust over. Luckily, someone else had taken the spill instead, and that someone was Marnie Fitzpatrick.

Since Mr. Quinn had witnessed their collision, Nola did the honorable thing and held her hand out to help Marnie up, but she just growled at Nola and pushed her hand away. After that, Nola marched out of the room, moodier and more hostile than ever. She couldn't believe

Marnie had the gall to encroach on her turf during their English presentation yesterday. Who did Marnie think she was all of a sudden? The fully rehabilitated and future do-gooder version of Paris Hilton? Nola could see through that thin veil from a mile away. Marnie may have thought that she could fool Nola with her fake altruism, but Nola knew better than to trust Marnie, despite one "nice" act. And if she could dodge her for the rest of her life, Nola figured she'd be happy.

However, when she arrived at the cafeteria, Nola realized that avoiding anyone would be absolutely out of the question. With the exception of one small, intimate dining experience on the bleachers, Nola had sat with Matt, Evan, and Iris every lunch period since the very first day of school. There was no way she could just sell her lunchtime real estate and relocate to Sally Applebaum's table or eat with the happy-go-lucky Tokers out in the parking lot without a lot of eyebrows being raised.

Nola didn't want any attention being drawn to her now, especially when rumors about her and Matt were probably bubbling up all over the place. So that meant she would have to go through the motions at the lunch table and clamp her mouth shut. As long as she kept her head down and didn't participate in any banter, Nola hoped that she'd be able to prevent ever-so-shy Evan from acknowledging his not-so-secret romantic feelings for her in the slightest bit.

Only that would prove to be excruciatingly difficult with Iris Santos's annoying blabbing habit thrown in the mix.

"So what's the deal with Homecoming, peeps?" Iris asked, cracking open a Diet Coke. "Are we skipping the dance altogether because *it's* lame or are we going as a group because *we're* lame? Let's discuss."

Nola bit into her grilled cheese sandwich and chewed ferociously so she wouldn't have to answer.

"I was planning on giving Riley the whole formal dance treatment. Limo ride, fancy dinner, elaborate wrist corsage, you name it," Matt said after biting into his meatball hero.

Iris pushed back her bangs and clipped them with a barrette that she plucked out of her purse. "What about you, Sanders? Have you pinned your hopes on some lucky dame?"

As soon as Evan's light green eyes gravitated toward Nola, she immediately looked down at her plate. It was conspicuous, yes, but better than having to withstand his fixed stare in front of an audience that included Matt Heatherly.

"I'm thinking of asking . . . *someone*," Nola heard Evan say in a soft whisper.

Oh, God, make it stop.

"*Someone*, eh?" Iris said mockingly. "Sounds promising, Ev."

When Nola glanced up a few seconds later, she saw that Evan had brought out his Sidekick and was typing on it frantically. Nola sighed in relief but kept her head lowered, just in case Evan gaped at her again.

Matt flung a potato chip in Iris's direction. "Well, has anyone asked you to the dance, Miss Santos?"

"Not yet, but that doesn't mean anything," Iris replied, and stuck out her tongue.

"Cute," Matt said, and threw another potato chip at her.

Iris turned to Nola. "All right, Nola. How's it looking between you and Ian the Hottie-Boombalottie?"

Nola had imagined on occasion what it might feel like if her heart ever stopped cold, but now she no longer had to wonder. She was thinking about motioning to her chest as if to signal Matt to perform CPR, but the oxygen to her brain had been severely compromised.

When Nola sat there frozen and didn't reply, Iris said, "That good, huh?"

Evan put his Sidekick in his front pocket, looked at

Matt, and shrugged his shoulders. "I have to be somewhere," he said sadly before slinking off.

Once Evan left the cafeteria, Matt threw a handful of potato chips at Iris, some of which caught in her silky black hair.

"Ugh! Why did you do that for?" Iris was far from amused.

"Because you have *such* a big mouth." Apparently, Matt wasn't in a laughing mood, either.

Iris peeled a greasy chip out of her long locks and sneered at Matt but didn't say anything else. Instead she got up in a huff and stormed off, presumably to the girls' bathroom. Nola was just thankful the near-death experience was over.

For now.

"Iris can be such a twit sometimes," Matt said in an attempt to console her.

"Do you really think Evan . . . will ask . . ." Nola's voice trailed off. Evan seemed like a nice enough guy, but he didn't even come close to being Matt. Still, it wasn't as though she had very many options in terms of a date. At least if she went with Evan, she might be able to have one slow dance with Matt.

"Like I said, Nola, he's shy city." Matt leaned back in his chair and pounded out a little rhythm on the table with his hands. "But I'm rooting for you two."

Even though she'd just imagined slow dancing with Matt under the dim lights of the gymnasium, now Nola wanted to flick him on the ear.

"A girl could do a lot worse than Evan, though," Matt added with a loud hand slap on the table. "Imagine ending up with Ian?" He made a grossed-out face and then winked at Nola.

Suddenly, Nola leaned over the table and flicked Matt like she'd never flicked her little brothers before.

"God, Nola! That hurt," Matt said, rubbing his left ear with his hand. "What'd you do that for?"

Nola had no idea what to say. In fact, she had no idea why Matt's comment about Ian sent her over the edge and into the flicking zone to begin with. The only thing she knew was that she needed to dodge Matt Heatherly for a while, so she picked up her things and left the cafeteria. Yet when she reached the hallway, Nola noticed that she didn't have anywhere else to go.

When Nola came home from school that day, the only thing she wanted to do was collect a bunch of her jewelry-making supplies from her precious window seat area, drag everything up to her room, and throw herself into a painstaking, thought-consuming project like a ten-foot-long necklace. It had looked as though she might be home free once she reached the top of the stairs, a Hobby House store bag filled to the top held tightly in her hand. But she was too frazzled to remember to check behind the door of her room as soon as she entered.

Nola had instituted this routine for a good reason. When she was twelve, Dennis and Dylan had gotten into the habit of hiding in her room right before she came home and jumping out from behind the door. Even when Nola knew it was coming, she'd still get startled enough to scream or drop whatever it was she was carrying.

Which was exactly what happened now.

"Annihilate her!" Dennis shrieked when he popped into view with a Nerf N-Strike.

"Dah!" Nola yelped, and then stumbled over Dylan, who was coming out from underneath her bed.

"Oh, no!" Dylan cried as he tried to prevent Nola from falling, but down she went, sending her bag spilling onto the carpet.

"Are you okay?" Dennis scurried over to Nola and helped her to her feet.

Nola looked down at all the beads that were scattered in the rug and her lower lip started to tremble. Not only would it take her forever to find every bead that was lost in the thick shag fabric, but she couldn't help but think of Marnie and how, if she were here, she would have kicked the boys out and rummaged through the carpet until she and Nola found every last little gem.

Nola was still pretty mad about Marnie's and her "Look how awesome I am! I just saved the day!" antics in yesterday's English class, but at times like these, even the kick-ass-and-take-names version of Nola was unable to dismiss her secret wish to have the old Marnie back as her best friend. Maybe then she wouldn't feel so overwhelmed and lonely.

Dylan's lower lip started to wobble when one of his sister's tears landed on his arm. "We're sorry, Nol. We didn't mean to hurt you."

"Here, we'll help clean it up." Dennis put down his play assault rifle and knelt on the floor. Dylan followed suit and started pulling out tiny stones from the carpet with his small hands.

Nola wiped at her eyes and smiled. If this had been a few weeks ago, the boys would have dashed out of the room, screaming, "I didn't do it!" This show of sibling solidarity was a very pleasant surprise. Could their change in demeanor have anything to do with . . .

"What happened here?"

Nola glimpsed at the door frame and there was Ian, dressed in a green crew-neck sweater that was a little too big for him and a pair of dark blue jeans, which were cuffed at the bottom so that the bright orange laces on his Pumas showed.

"We had an accident," Dylan said without taking his eyes off the rug.

Ian smirked when he saw the Nerf weapon lying by Dennis's feet. "Why am I finding that hard to believe, Den?"

Dennis, always the defiant one, stood up and challenged him. "But it was, Ian! We apologized and everything. Ask Nola."

"Is that true, Nol?" Ian asked.

"Yes, they did apologize. And they were cleaning up, too," she answered.

"Well, that's good to hear." Ian clapped his hands together three times, and the boys stood up straight as though they were in the military. "Okay, guys, head downstairs and play quietly while I help Nola."

"Yes, Ian," Dennis and Dylan said in unison.

When her little brothers scampered away, Nola froze in shock for the second time in less than twelve hours. How did Ian manage to get the twins to *listen* to him, let alone *obey* him?

"Are you using hypnotism on them or something?" Nola asked, completely agog.

Ian pushed up the sleeves of his sweater and squatted

down so he could take a closer look at the carpet. "I'll never tell you," he replied with a self-satisfied grin.

Nola sat cross-legged on the floor next to him and smirked. "I guess I won't subject you to an interrogation, then."

"So you were planning on making something tonight, huh?" Ian said as he took a few beads and put them in his cupped hand.

"Yeah, I was. Didn't know what yet, but I just wanted to take my mind off things." Nola wanted to slap herself after saying that. Telling Ian about her issues wasn't the best idea, especially when it came to . . .

"Are you having trouble with that guy who keeps coming over?" Suddenly, Ian stopped what he was doing and looked into Nola's eyes. It was weird — usually Nola recoiled when Ian took this overprotective tone with her, but tonight, she found it kind of . . . endearing.

"You mean . . . Matt?"

There was that strange feeling again. When she said Matt's name, her shoulders immediately tensed up.

"Sure, whatever," Ian said with a pompous eye roll.

And now the recoiling instinct was back!

"Never mind, Ian," Nola said gruffly. "I can handle my own problems."

"Fine."

"Fine!"

A frustrated Nola quickly leaned over to grab a purple bead, but so did Ian. Their foreheads bumped so hard, she saw spots and stars floating in front of her eyes.

"Ow!" Nola called out as she massaged her head with her hand.

"Man, that *killed!*" Ian moaned.

Once Nola's vision came back to normal, she peered at Ian, who was hiding his face with his hands. After she saw the small goose egg that was forming on his head, Nola started to giggle. Something this ridiculous could only happen with Ian.

"Gee, I thought you had a much harder noggin than that," she teased.

Ian tried not to snicker, but his efforts were futile. "It's no match for yours, apparently."

Nola laughed but acted as though she was insulted. "Are you trying to say that *I'm* thickheaded?"

She leaned forward to swat Ian on the shoulder, but she flinched when he grabbed her hand and pulled her so close to him that his nose was practically grazing hers. Nola's breathing became shallow and sporadic, like she was about to hyperventilate. She'd never been so excited and scared at the same time . . . and by some-one other than Matt Heatherly.

"I'm trying to say that you're beautiful," Ian mur-mured, right before turning his head a little, closing his eyes, and pressing his lips lightly against Nola's.

At first, Nola didn't kiss him back. Her eyes were wide open like a stunned animal that was about to get smacked by a dump truck. But when it began to register that Ian tasted like butterscotch and how soft his hands felt against her face and how her heart was galloping galloping galloping, Nola closed her eyes and kissed Ian, too.

Soon, she was running her fingers through his hair, which felt like feathers against her warming skin. Ian pulled back a little, his lower lip just touching her top lip, his hand tracing the outline of Nola's chin. Then suddenly he pulled back *a lot*. Nola stared into his eyes while she caught her breath, her thoughts raining down on her like pieces of confetti.

Why did Ian kiss me? Why did Ian stop kissing me?

Nola could see from Ian's dazed expression that he didn't know, either, which explained why he got up and left Nola's room, quietly closing the door behind him.

Chapter 24

If you received this note in your locker, then you are
one of a few select people invited to attend a secret-
password inauguration party held in honor of
freshman class treasurer Marnie Fitzpatrick. Reply via
e-mail to the address below and you will be given the
password and location. DO NOT TELL ANYONE
YOU HAVE THIS NOTE! ALL POSEURS WILL BE
PROSECUTED TO THE FULLEST EXTENT OF
THE LAW!

On Friday night, Marnie checked out her reflection in
the full-length mirror in Grier's bedroom. She had to
admit she was looking mighty . . . boss, whatever the
hell that meant. Anyway, if the word had replaced
fierce in Lizette's slang-onary, then Marnie had to
assume that being boss was a very, very good thing.

Marnie rubbed a bit of Pantene styling gel into her
roots and flipped her head over and back so that she
could attain maximum volume. Then she tugged down
the waistband of her Blue Cult jeans (not hers, really,
but on loan from Grier) and straightened her sunburst-
colored jewel-tie halter top (which she bought at Wet
Seal yesterday and ripped off the tag the moment she

got home). After that, she retouched her makeup, applying another layer of Too Faced blush on her cheeks.

When she finished primping, Marnie took another long, hard look at herself. Here she was, minutes away from her big inauguration bash, where she'd be showered with attention and adored by Majors, just like she'd always wanted. Only now that she stared into her own dimming, sad eyes, Marnie wasn't even sure if she wanted to go downstairs and meet the crowd of special guests that was already forming in Grier's monster-size, hooked-up living room.

It was Lizette's idea to keep Marnie upstairs until everyone arrived so she could make a big entrance, but Marnie wished that she could just sneak off into the night and go someplace where there wouldn't be any pressure. She sat down on Grier's queen-size canopy bed, which was covered in lacy fabrics and pretty floral patterns, and did a series of neck rolls, hoping this would calm her anxiety. After five minutes, all hope was lost. Considering how much stress was weighing on her, Marnie wasn't going to be able to get herself out of this funk with that simplistic maneuver.

Marnie wasn't left with another choice. She had to resort to a more serious form of relaxation technique or present herself to her loyal constituents with the rigidity of a robot instead of the gracefulness of a ballerina.

Despite the voice screaming "Don't do it!" in her head, Marnie got up, went to the center of Grier's room, and prepared to do an intermediate yoga pose — *unsupervised.*

Marnie had seen Lizette do the Plough at YogaWorks a week or so ago, and although Marnie hadn't been to another class, she'd been working on her flexibility since then, stretching in the mornings when she woke up and at night before she went to bed. Marnie remembered exactly how Lizette bent her body. She would have to be really careful and take her time in order to replicate it, but she felt that if she mastered this, even for a brief moment, she'd have control over her increasingly complicated life.

Marnie kicked off her plaid Keds skimmers and lay down on Grier's soft off-white carpet. This pose called for Marnie to lift both legs so that they made a ninety-degree angle with her body. Then she'd have to slowly lower her legs over her head so that her back arched fully and her toes almost touched the floor.

You can do this, Marn. Just concentrate. Focus. Think Plough.

Marnie inhaled deeply and raised both of her legs in unison. Once she contorted herself into a ninety-degree angle, she exhaled. Then she lifted her hips and braced her lower back with her hands so that she could gingerly bring her legs down over her head. This proved to be a difficult task, though, and not because of Marnie's lack of elasticity. The jeans that Marnie borrowed from Grier were compressing her thighs to the point were she was afraid the seams would burst, and now that Marnie was attempting the Plough, that might actually happen.

Marnie gasped for air as her legs dangled above her. She wasn't sure if she should abandon the pose quickly or try to ease out of it. Either one could cause irreparable damage to Grier's precious denim and Marnie's slightly less precious spine. She would have deliberated a little bit longer, but she got distracted when a pair of buffed, brown Kenneth Cole loafers came into view.

Even though she was staring at them upside down, Marnie knew they belonged to none other than Dane Harris.

"When Lizette said you were up in Grier's room waiting for an escort, I never would have imagined this."

Suddenly, Marnie's fulcrum gave way and her body crumbled to the side, landing hard on Grier's floor.

Damn it! And oooouuuuucchhhhh!

Dane rushed over to Marnie and knelt down next to her. "Are you okay?"

"I'm fine," Marnie lied. She felt a burning sensation

at the back of her left leg, which probably indicated a torn ligament or something.

"Good, because Grier's place is packed." Dane took Marnie by the hands and helped her to her feet. When she regained her equilibrium, Marnie nearly lost it again at the sight of Dane, decked out in a fabulous-looking pair of dark blue Seven jeans and a black short-sleeved button-down top made out of a soft fabric that also shimmered a little bit.

Hold on, I *am going to the Homecoming dance with this smoking-hot guy? I've got to be the luckiest girl* on the freaking planet*!*

"You should leave the life-threatening tricks to your stunt double, sweetheart," Dane joked, right before delivering the most perfectly gentle kiss on Marnie's lips.

Marnie wobbled on her feet a little afterward. How was Dane able to make her lightheaded just by kissing her?

"I know. I was nervous, so I thought that yoga might relax me, that's all."

"Did it work?" Dane smirked.

"Nope," Marnie said, giggling.

Dane rubbed her bare arms softly. "Well, what do you have to be nervous about?"

Marnie scribbled down a list in her head, but once she got to the fifth item—which was humiliating

Sawyer in front of Lizette yesterday — she was mentally exhausted.

"Nothing, really," she finally replied.

"Good." Dane put his warm hand on Marnie's flushed cheek, making it almost impossible for her to think that he'd even look at another girl, even Lizette. "Tonight is your night to shine."

Marnie wanted to take comfort in Dane's reassurances, but she still couldn't shake this nagging sense of worry that started the second after Sawyer slunk off down the hall yesterday. Or maybe it was even before then, when Brynne got up in her grille after her student council meeting, or when she went to Stewart's to see Nola, only to find her ex-boyfriend, Weston, waiting there for her. Right now, it was hard to trace this off-kilter feeling back to its roots.

"Shall we meet your public, Madame Treasurer?" Dane said with a goofy, overdone aristocratic accent.

"Why, yes, indeed we shall." Marnie's accent wasn't as good as Dane's, but being silly with him eased her mind some.

As Marnie descended Grier's marble staircase with Dane on her arm, she felt her stomach fluttering with excitement. There was an enormous crowd of people gathered at the base of the stairs, and when they burst into applause, her anxiety drifted away like a tiny message in a teeny bottle on the grand open sea.

Marnie replied to the cheers with a modest wave and a glorious smile while Dane led her to a small space in the center of the living room, where more partygoers were assembled to hear from the hostess. Lizette had told Marnie that she'd be waiting there so she could give a rousing speech, but as Marnie and others glanced around, she realized that Lizette was not among Marnie's dedicated voters.

"Has anyone seen Zee?" Marnie asked no one in particular.

"I think she's in the kitchen," she heard a voice call out.

"Thanks, be right back," Marnie replied, and slipped out of the limelight and into Grier's professional-grade kitchen, which was filled with state-of-the-art stainless steel appliances and a pot rack that dangled from the ceiling.

Before Marnie pushed through the swinging white door, she was expecting to see Lizette grabbing a bottle of champagne for the toast. But that's not what was on the other side at all. Instead Marnie was face-to-face-to-face-to-face with Lizette, Brynne, and Grier, who were shooting her the nastiest glares she'd witnessed since her fifth viewing of *Mean Girls*.

"What's wrong, guys?" Marnie said, her voice cracking.

Lizette's cute stewardess-inspired outfit and pigtails couldn't outdo the furious look in her eyes. "What's *wrong*? I can't believe you have the nerve to even ask me that."

Marnie immediately shifted her gaze toward the evil gap-toothed Brynne, who was smiling like she'd just eaten a defenseless stray cat.

Oh, she didn't. She couldn't have. I've been kissing her ass, and I didn't even tell Principal Baxter about the posters!

Marnie bit her lower lip and wrung her hands behind her back. She was fumbling around in her mind for something to say but figured the best way to stall was to feign ignorance. "I don't know what you mean."

Lizette took a few gruff steps toward Marnie and poked her hard in the shoulder.

Okay, maybe ignorance wasn't the way to go.

"You've been messing around with Sawyer *behind my back*?" Lizette shouted.

Grier padded up behind Lizette. Marnie was hoping she'd say something sweet and diffuse the situation like she normally did, but from the stern look on Grier's face, it was clear whose back she had. "Brynne told us *everything*. How could you, Marnie?"

Marnie was never quite sure if she had it in her to

hate someone. Even when she was upset and angry at Nola, Marnie couldn't bring herself to actually *hate* her ex-best friend. But now she realized hating someone was possible, and she hated Brynne Callaway with a vengeance. Thankfully, this hate gave Marnie the power and courage to expose Brynne for who she really was — a double-crossing, no-good, filthy liar.

"Zee, Brynne is making this whole thing up," Marnie said, throwing Brynne a sharp dagger of a sneer. "She's just jealous and wants to see me sweat. End of story."

Brynne didn't move or even say a word. She was too busy enjoying the show.

"So you deny being at the skate park with Sawyer?" Lizette challenged her.

"I saw him there, yes, but —"

"And the two of you weren't going at it like crazy, like Brynne said you were?"

"*No!* Of course not! We were just —"

"Someone else confirmed Brynne's story, Marnie," Grier snapped.

Marnie felt as though she'd been kicked in the head with her own steel-toed boots. "Who?"

"*We* have our sources." Lizette took a few steps back and put her arm around Brynne.

It must be the demon's little spy.

Marnie was certain she was going to puke, so she

grabbed Grier's arm for some support, but Grier whipped it away and joined her friends at the other end of the kitchen.

"I think *you* and your party are *oh*-ver," Brynne said, leering at Marnie like a grade-A psychopath.

It was true — for Marnie, this party was most definitely over. Now that Lizette thought she was a traitor, there was no way Marnie could stick around and sneak out to the mansion with Dane and dance the night away with her new gaggle of friends. Marnie wanted to punch Brynne's lights out and convince Lizette that she was innocent, but as she looked at the three of them through watery eyes, she could see that her sister, Erin, had been right — Marnie was dispensable. The girls' arms were linked together, making an invincible fortress that would force Marnie out of Grier's house and out of the Majors so quickly that she wouldn't even get a chance to say good-bye to Dane.

Once the front door of Grier's house had slammed in her face, Marnie remembered her brutal altercation with Nola at Deirdre Boyd's party. When Nola had scampered away from her that evening, Marnie had felt a rush of adrenaline and excitement after shaming her old friend who she believed had done her wrong. As she wandered down the driveway, tears streaking her cheeks, Marnie realized how the tables had turned. Now, she was in Nola's position — humiliated and shunned because of a false accusation — and the only rush of emotion she could feel at the moment was despair.

Who could she possibly turn to in the wake of this disaster?

"Marnie, are you okay?"

Somehow she had wandered to the corner of Grier's street, although she didn't quite know how she got there. But she did know the sound of that voice, which belonged to Weston Briggs.

Marnie wiped at her eyes but she was so choked up she couldn't respond.

Weston shoved his hands in his pockets and leaned back on his heels, obviously uncomfortable with the situation. "Does the party suck *that* bad?"

Marnie almost managed to giggle, but her anguish was so immense that she threw her arms around Weston and started to sob hysterically. She didn't care if he thought she was a lunatic. Marnie needed someone to hold on to desperately, and since Weston was standing right there, she figured he'd do.

However, Marnie didn't expect Weston to put his arms around her, too, and whisper, "Everything is going to be all right."

It might not have been true, but as Marnie had learned tonight, the truth was hard to come by in high school.

Chapter 25

On Saturday morning, Nola was eating her blueberry pancakes over the kitchen sink while her father tried to get the boys to stop squirting each other over the oak table with the organic maple syrup bottle. He tried a variety of tactics to get them to quit misbehaving, including a not very convincing list of threats. As Nola chewed her food slowly while peering down at her plate, she reminded herself that she had *kissed* the only person who could get the twins to submit with three claps of his amazingly smooth hands.

Not that Nola needed reminding. Since Ian had kissed her yesterday afternoon (at precisely 4:38 P.M., in fact), the taste of butterscotch was still on her lips. Even the syrup on her pancakes couldn't get rid of it. Actually, Nola was hoping to savor the flavor of her first real, non–Truth or Dare kiss for as long as possible. Although Marnie had always gushed about how fabulous it was to kiss Weston, Nola hadn't really thought about smooching any boy until she met Matt. And truth be told, when Ian was kissing her tenderly last night, Matt hadn't even entered her mind once.

Still, Nola hadn't seen or talked to Ian since he had left her room without saying so much as a "See ya later."

Sure, Nola had locked her door, jacked up the volume on her iDeck, and hid in her closet until this morning, but she was positive that had nothing to do with Ian throwing on the brakes and disappearing on her. Nola was certain that Ian had regretted indulging his sudden and fleeting urge to kiss her so much that she wondered — or was it worried? — if he might never kiss her *again*.

As fate would have it, though, the moment she felt some sticky goo spray into her hair, all Nola could think about were the ways in which she could inflict the most pain on her little brothers.

Nola set her plate on the counter and spun around with her butter knife. "Okay! *Who* did that?!"

Instantly, Dennis and Dylan pointed at each other and then sprinted into the living room.

"Put the knife down, Nola," her dad said firmly. "If anyone is going to punish them, it will be me."

"Please tell me the punishment will involve *cutlery*." Nola gnashed her teeth.

Mr. James pried the knife out of Nola's death grip and put a calming hand on her shoulder. "It's only syrup. It'll come out with some shampoo."

Nola mumbled something under her breath and stalked over to the refrigerator for some orange juice. She reached for the carton and felt that it was almost empty.

"God, can't *anything* go right in my life?" she cried, slamming the refrigerator door closed.

Nola's dad pulled a chair out from the kitchen table. "I think you and I ought to talk."

She flopped down in the chair with a scowl on her face. "Talk about what?"

"About this mood you've been in lately," her father said.

"I don't know what you mean." Nola mindlessly ran a finger over a scratch in the surface of the wood.

"Well, I haven't seen you sulk this much since your mother and I said no to that pony you begged for."

Nola couldn't suppress a small grin. She and Marnie had been obsessed with horses in the third grade. They'd read every book in the Thoroughbred series, and Marnie's mom would sometimes take them to Hidden Pond Stables so they could watch the trainers ride their horses.

That seems so long ago.

Nola's father sat in a chair next to her and looked at her with loving eyes. "Listen, your mom told me what happened with Marnie. I know you must be feeling bad now, but yelling at everyone isn't going to solve anything."

Nola rolled her eyes. She doubted her dad understood what she'd been going through. Losing her best friend was just one of the problems that had buried her like an avalanche.

"Things will work out between you two, you just need to give it some time. Being patient is hard, I know, but it sure beats being angry."

"I'm sorry, Dad." Nola leaned back in her chair and retied the belt on her bathrobe so it was tight around her waist. "I'm just —"

"Being a typical teenager?" Her dad mussed up her sticky hair and smiled. "I only wanted to let you know that I'm here for you and that you can come talk to me about anything. Okay?"

Nola nodded halfheartedly. Her dad made it sound so easy, but what were the chances that she'd knock on the door to his home office one evening and tell him about her amazing kiss with the boy he was paying to watch his kids? Less than one in a zillion. The person best equipped to handle that kind of secret information was a best friend.

However, the girl who had lived up to that definition for years was now her sworn enemy. Given that they couldn't even stand to look at each other, how would being patient ever bring Nola and Marnie back together again? It sounded like a crazy yet well-intentioned theory that only a father would dream up.

"I saved the comics for you, like always." Mr. James

pushed the *Poughkeepsie Journal* across the table and set it in front of Nola. "It looks like it's been through a tree sap factory, though. You still want to read it?"

"Sure," she replied. Reading the newspaper on Saturday mornings was one of Nola's favorite things to do. Marnie used to tease her about it relentlessly, though, which is why she had to pretend that she only read it for the *Charlie Brown* and *Calvin and Hobbes* strips.

"Good. I'll go find the boys," her father said.

"Just follow the trail of syrup," Nola said with a weak laugh.

"Thanks for the tip." Her dad patted her on the back affectionately and went on the hunt.

Nola flipped through the first two pages of the world news section of the paper before getting to a page that was covered in brown maple goo. She made a disgusted face and then put the section on the chair next to her. Nola inspected the community section thoroughly this time. Once she saw that there were no hidden messes, she started at the front page and began to read. The first article at the top was about local property taxes going up. She lost interest after the second paragraph, so she glanced down to the article beneath it. The headline caught her eye:

**MISSING PERSONS CASE
REOPENS IN BINGHAMTON**

Nola leaned over the paper, her elbows on the table and her chin in her hands. Even though she hated mystery-themed birthday parties, she loved true-crime stories and was engrossed after reading the first line.

> Five years ago, a 34-year-old woman left
> work at Lockheed Martin and never returned
> home to her husband and son.

Nola thought for a moment about what it would be like if her mother disappeared, and an intense chill ripped through her. Despite her discomfort, she kept reading.

> Binghamton police had been doggedly inves-
> tigating the case, but a lack of solid physical
> evidence caused them to halt their search in
> November 2004.

One of Nola's favorites TV shows was *Dateline NBC*, so she was immediately suspicious of this woman's husband. In situations like these, the spouse was always the main suspect.

> Last week, in a surprising turn of events,
> detectives uncovered the missing woman's
> 2003 Toyota Corolla at a camping site in rural
> Elmira.

Nola raised her eyebrows with deep interest.

> They hope that this break in the case will lead

them to the whereabouts of Binghamton
native Diane Heatherly.

When Nola read the name of the missing woman,
her chin slipped out of her hands and the arches of her
size eight-and-a-half feet began to sweat.

Nola skipped ahead a few sentences, her pulse
shooting up a few notches with each word that she
scanned. Finally, her eyes locked onto a passage that
made her gasp out loud.

> Diane's husband, Michael Heatherly, cur-
> rently a session musician based in
> Poughkeepsie, has been previously quoted in
> the Binghamton *Press & Sun-Bulletin* as say-
> ing he believed his wife had decided to leave
> him, but that their son, Matthew, was
> convinced that she'd been abducted. So
> Heatherly filed a missing person report when
> his wife didn't come home for three days.
> Now it appears that their son was right.

After reading that paragraph, Nola's throat became
dry and scratchy. She couldn't believe that this was what
Matt had been hiding. All the disappearances, all the
awkward moments, all the secrets from his past were
most likely linked to this one tragic event in his life.
Why didn't he ever tell her?

Suddenly, the dryness and scratchiness in her throat spread throughout her body. Her skin felt as though someone had lit a match and set her on fire. Then Nola recalled how she'd angrily flicked Matt's ear yesterday, and her stomach tied into a hundred knots.

Oh, my God, I'm such a jerk!

Nola sprang up from her chair and tore the article out of the paper. Without thinking or realizing she was still in her pajamas and bathrobe, she ran to the hallway closet and shoved her feet into her Skechers. Then she dashed out of the house and went to find the one person who could help her get to Ridge Road, no questions asked.

Acknowledgments

As always, I'd like to thank the stellar, talented, and oh-so-beautiful team at Scholastic/Point who make writing the IN OR OUT series a true joy: Aimee Friedman, Abigail McAden, Sheila Marie Everett, and Morgan Matson. Of course, I couldn't have achieved anything without the support of my family and good friends — I love you all so much. Extra-special appreciation goes out to Katzuji Kawasaki, who is not only a spectacular cousin but a first-rate bookseller and promoter — you're the best, Kaz! And to my readers, thanks for your e-mails and embracing Nola and Marnie as you have. I couldn't be more grateful.

Take a sneak peek at

FRIENDS CLOSE, ENEMIES CLOSER
An IN or OUT novel

"Honey, I'm about to take off," Marnie's mother called from outside the bathroom door.

Marnie had managed to sneak into the house yesterday without running into her mom, so Mrs. Fitzpatrick had no idea that her daughter had been recently punted into the far reaches of the socially ostracized section of the popularity playing field.

"Okay," Marnie replied weakly

"Do you need anything from the outside world?" her mom asked.

A new life would be nice.

"No, I'm fine." Marnie glanced at the mirror and saw that she still appeared as though she'd narrowly escaped a dogfight.

"Alright then. I quess I'll just bring Erin straight home after I pick her up from the train station."

A sharp pain shot up from her stomach and lodged in the back of her head. Marnie had forgotten that her sister would be coming to stay for a while so that she could pass down her crown at the Poughkeepsie Central Homecoming dance, among the duties the former queen was expected to perform. How was Marnie supposed to deal with her goddess of a sister when a freaking million-ton asteriod had just struck her once-perfect world?

Once Marnie heard her mom's Corolla pull out of the driveway, she emerged from the bathroom a soggy, wrinkled mess of a girl. She trudged to her bedroom, threw on a cute pair of purple plaid lounge pants and a ribbed pink tank that she scored on gojane.com, and put her hair up in a slick ponytail. She was about to crawl back under the covers and lie there until the dawn of a new civilization, but, her Razr phone had other ideas. Marnie's heart fluttered for a moment when she heard the Rihanna ringtone, but once she recalled whom that tune belonged to, she wanted nothing more than to throw her cell out the window.

Marnie picked up without even saying hello.

"Where's Mom? I've been waiting for her, like, a minute already!" The sound of her sister's high-pitched voice had no trouble exceeding the volume of the noisy bustle of the train station.

"She just left," Marnie said, sighing.

"Ugh! Typical," Erin replied snottily.

Marnie's jaw stiffened so much she wasn't sure she'd be able to utter another word. "Is that all? I have things to do."

"Yeah, right. Oh, and Marnie, my closet better be just as I left it. Got that?" her sister snapped before hanging up.

Marnie did resort to throwing her phone, but it just hit the mountains of pillows on her bed.

Quickly, she made her way down the stairs and into the kitchen, hoping that she could scarf down some food before her mom returned with Erin the Evil. As she rustled through the cupboards in search of a box of Frosted Flakes, Marnie chastised herself for being such a coward. Here she was scambling around like a frightened squirrel so she could lock herself in her room to mope without coming into contact with Erin. This wasn't the same Marnie who had won class treasurer and made out with the hottest, most desirable guy in her high school and hobnobbed with the coolest kids in

Poughkeepsie's upper-echelon! In fact, now that Marnie thought about it, she was acting like . . .

Her perpetually terrified, hive-ridden ex-best friend Nola James. Or at least the version of Nola she knew prior to Nola's metamorphosis into an angry dictator.

Marnie froze when this realizaton sunk in, her eyes fixated on Tony the Tiger's. Thankfully, the ding-dong of the doorbell shook her loose of his trance.

She set the box of cereal down on the countertop and scooted across the kitchen linoleum with bare, but well-pedicured, feet. Marnie opened the door, half expecting to see the Sunday paper strewn about on the porch—the Fitzpatricks had the tardiest delivery person in the neighborhood. Yet she wished she'd been visited by the Angel of Death when it dawned on her she was standing in front of the aforementioned hottest guy in her high school, looking as though she'd just crawled out from under a few piles of Sheetrock.

"Hey," Dane Harris said as he pushed up the sleeves of his shirt.

To Do List: Read all the Point books!

By Aimee Friedman

❏ South Beach

❏ French Kiss

❏ Hollywood Hills

❏ The Year My Sister Got Lucky

❏ Oh Baby!
By Randi Reisfeld and H.B. Gilmour

❏ Hotlanta
By Denene Millner and Mitzi Miller

By Hailey Abbott

❏ Summer Boys

❏ Next Summer: A Summer Boys Novel

❏ After Summer: A Summer Boys Novel

❏ Last Summer: A Summer Boys Novel

By Claudia Gabel

❏ In or Out

❏ Loves Me, Loves Me Not: An In or Out Novel

❏ Sweet and Vicious: An In or Out Novel

By Nina Malkin

❏ 6X: The Uncensored Confessions

❏ 6X: Loud, Fast, & Out of Control

❏ Orange Is the New Pink

By Jeanine Le Ny

❏ Once Upon a Prom: Date

❏ Once Upon a Prom: Dress

❏ Once Upon a Prom: Dream